OTHER WORKS BY DAVID MAMET

Some Freaks

Writing In Restaurants

The Village

On Directing Film

The Cabin

Make-Believe Town

Three Uses of the Knife

Passover

True and False

The
Old
Religion

David
Mamet

THE FREE PRESS

New York   London   Toronto

Sydney   Singapore

THE FREE PRESS
A Division of Simon & Schuster Inc.
1230 Avenue of the Americas
New York, NY 10020

THE FREE PRESS and colophon are trademarks
of Simon & Schuster Inc.

Designed by Carla Bolte

Manufactured in the United States of America

10   9   8   7   6   5   4   3   2   1

Library of Congress Cataloging-in-Publication Data

Mamet, David.
     The old religion : a novel / David Mamet.
         p.   cm.
     ISBN 0-684-84119-3
     I.   Title.
PS3563.A4345O39   1997
813'.54—dc21   97-17854
                                         CIP

פֿאר דער סודבעריער רבי

This book is dedicated to

Rabbi Larry Kushner

A crucible for silver, a furnace for gold,
and the Lord tries hearts.

—Proverbs 17:3

The
Old
Religion

In 1915 a young factory girl was killed in Atlanta, Georgia. Her name was Mary Phagan, and she worked at the National Pencil Factory. The factory manager was Leo Frank. He was a New York Jew. Frank was accused of the crime and brought to trial.

Preparing for the trip
to Morris's house

The newspaper lined a bandbox. He opened the band-box to get a fresh shirt collar. He wondered, as he often did, at the appearance of the newspaper. It had been glued into the sides and bottom of the box, and the date showed April 10, 1868. But the newsprint had not yellowed. "Obviously the glue is a preservative," he thought.

"We might think what there is in the glue to preserve the clarity, and, so, arrive at a new process, or, at a new application of an existing operation to lengthen the life of newsprint." He smiled.

"But is not longevity in opposition to its very nature, which is *temporareity?* And *if* we had begun with newsprint which resisted time, would it not be an advancement if, by extraction of the preservative glue, the cost or difficulty of manufacture could decrease? If some man," he thought, "recognized one day it was not *necessary* for the print to retain clarity beyond the one day, and, so doing, reformed the industry . . . ?

"Yes," he thought. "Yes. You could take it either the one way or the other. And either would be as astounding."

The newsprint advertised, along the fold where the box's sides and bottom met, a meeting to petition Isabella, the queen of Spain, for the release of Edgardo Mortara.

"Restore the Child to its Rightful Parents . . . ," the print read. It was a sheet of the *Brooklyn Eagle,* and had been glued into the box by someone in his wife's family, back in those days.

Edgardo Mortara was a Jewish child. He'd fallen ill and was believed near death.

One day, in his parents' absence, his Catholic nurse took him from the house and had him baptized, to save his soul. The child was kidnapped by the state—taken from his parents' home. No diplomatic or religious pressure was sufficient to induce the government of Spain or the Catholic church to give the child back.

Frank looked down at the clipping and thought of the discussions, the endless and not unenjoyable discussions, he and his fellow Jews had had about the outrage.

The bandbox held his collars and, in a soft morocco

purse, his collar studs. He fitted the collar into his clean shirt and stepped to the mirror to tie his tie.

"Yes, you look nice," his wife said.

He nodded, and they continued to prepare for the ritual trip to Morris's house.

Morris tells a story about Southern Jews

Morris spoke: " . . . you see, with the placards of the Klan and the announcements—do you see, they put it in the local paper: 'Jews and Catholics. You are not required. Leave now or be eliminated.'

"Well, in Belton, Renston, that area, now, they're dragging people from their homes. Some priest . . . " He coughed.

He leaned forward and took a sip of the cordial.

"D'you get these glasses from?" he said.

"Aunt Claire," Frank said.

"Gave 'em to you . . . ?"

"Certainly did."

He admired the small, etched glass, and turned it to the light, and raised it to examine the base.

"Czechoslovakia," he read. He sighed and leaned back into the davenport, resting his left arm out along its high wooden frame.

" . . . Czechoslovakia," he said, softly, to himself, content that it meant nothing, content to be the head of the family, to be a man, happy with his friends, relaxed and full of a good dinner, and to be serious in the way people are when the subject is arguably more personal than gossip but devoid of any real threat—who are entertained by those best of entertainments, which go by the name of serious business.

"I don't begrudge him," Frank thought. "He is, upon balance, fair, and no more pompous than I would be in his situation—than I, in all probability, am now.

"If we prize substance, then he, as a substantial man, is worthy of admiration.

"And, by God, given time, and with a little help, I might accomplish as much as he."

"The Ku Klux Klan," Morris began again.

" . . . But, finally, who does he think he is?" Frank thought.

"The Ku Klux Klan. Which of us is immune?" Morris said.

"For all the world like bugbear stories around a campfire," Frank thought.

"And don't we sit here with our eyes wide like ten-year-old children—thrilled to be frightened?"

Mayra came back into the room, and behind her,

Frank saw the colored maid, who, it was obvious, had just been receiving some timely instructions from her.

Mayra stood in the doorway and looked out on her husband as he continued. She looked down over her family, so still, listening to Morris go on.

She settled herself into the chair by the door. Slowly, in the rhythm of his speech, sinking down. Her husband, his eyes in a sweep of the assemblage, caught her eye and nodded, as if to a prized lieutenant.

"... and so *Weiss* . . . ," he said.

One of the children ran through the hall on some errand, and her mother reached out of the parlor and drew her in and whispered to her.

"... stayed at his home. Three days. And waited the ax blow."

One of the men nodded, and expelled the cigar smoke.

"... in all anxiety. His *store*. His *home*."

"His savings . . . ," one cousin said.

"Well, *exactly*," Morris said. "Exactly," granting the man's intrusion grandly.

"His wife and family. Afraid to venture to the store. The store shuttered. The help . . . I don't know if the household help came in, those days. They did not say. I *do* know they were bound to the house. The family. And whomever was there.

"What *fantasies*," he said, as he took up the main theme again, "must not have formed in his mind? Of flight . . . of opposition . . . What was he to do? I don't believe he even had a shotgun in the house. In fact, I'm sure he didn't."

The men in the room nodded.

"Of flight, then? Abandoning everything? And how to flee? If the Klan ruled the roads? And could they go cross-country? Now. What did that leave?"

"The railroad," a young boy suggested.

The adults looked at him.

"No. No. That's right," Morris said. "That left the railroad. And they packed those few things they thought they could carry without attracting undue attention—as casual travelers might carry. And they planned to walk out, on Saturday evening, as if for a stroll, do you see, to the depot. Timing their walk to coincide with the departure—mind you, not the arrival, but the departure—of the nine-eighteen to Corinth.

"For they would not want to appear and to board the train, only to have the Klan board after them, and drag them from it. How terrible *that* would be—so close to freedom . . ."

He looked down at the cordial glass on the table before him. He reached forward and pushed it gently, by the base, so gently forward three inches.

"They took a baby carriage," he said. "Scheming to save those few things it would hold. A wicker baby carriage filled with the silver, this photograph or that, *I* don't know, *papers* . . .

"And, at the time they set off . . ."

"All over the town: posters. 'The Knights of the Ku Klux Klan vow death upon the Scourge of Mankind, the Catholic and the Jew. And will eliminate them from our Midst, and stand, like the fiery ever-turning Sword . . .'"

"Well, I think that the State Militia should have come," a young cousin said. "And yes, and yes, 'Who *is* the State Militia,' but it seems to me . . ."

"It seems to you what?" Morris said. "It seems to you *what?* What does it seem to you?" He smiled.

"What *happened* to them?" one of the women said, and the group rustled and settled themselves again toward Morris.

"Well, I'm going to tell you," he said. "They set out, walking down to the depot. Thinking at any moment to receive a bullet in the head, a rifle butt to the face, a *shout* which said, 'There are the Jews!'

"To be dragged into an alley; into the town *square.* And they walked on. Past the store. They glanced at it, 'Weiss's Dry Goods.'

"The store they had built from nothing: his father a peddler, a pack on his back.

"And now Weiss. A pillar of the town. Who has a cause? A donation required, a . . ."

The men nodded. Businessmen.

". . . a gift of . . . a bolt of *cloth.* The *uniforms* . . ."

"That's right," one of the cousins said.

". . . for the *ball* teams. For the band. *Community* work, call it what you will. Who do they come to? A part of the town for the years, fifty years, that they had been there. 'Weiss. Dry Goods.' And here is the town. Risen against them, and one *shout* for blood, and their bodies swinging in the wind. As they walked past the store.

"And you can imagine his bitterness—to pass the store, knowing at any moment and *inevitably* it will be broken into, plundered. Burnt, no doubt. A shell. And what were two generations of his family's life?

"They heard the whistle of the train, come into the town. As they walked on now.

"They walked on. They crossed the square. There was the Klan, down the Main Street. There was a rally, and they'd thrown up a small platform, and there they were, in the Robes of the Inquisition were up there, haranguing the crowd. Thirty, fifty men now, in their white robes, and the crowd of the townspeople.

"Well. They are committed. And they proceed to the train. What was that out of the side of his eye? Does Weiss see one of the Klansmen turn and spy him? Yes. No. What?

"On they walk. Do you see the pathetic procession? Man and wife. And three children, and a baby carriage, in which is all they have salvaged of their life.

"There is the depot. And there is the train. And people boarding. And there is the conductor, that's right, checking his watch. Looks up the line, looks back; and is about to wave the brakeman to pull out. As the family comes up, comes up to the train, hurrying now: 'Get on board.' Weiss has his family board—he will go last, taking the baby carriage, and can still *hear*, do you see, the speaker and the crowd but one street over. 'Cleanse our Land in Blood. . . . Death to the vermin . . . Death to those who *bring* death. . . . Death to the Jews. . . . '

"About to board the train. 'Praise God I have gotten my family away from this.'

"When there is a hand on his shoulder. And he turns to see three of the hooded men."

The colored girl was coming in with a new pot of coffee. Mayra, seated near the kitchen, put her hand out to stay her.

". . . And Weiss turned to see the three men."

"'Where are you going?' the one says.

"Can he make his voice out? Does Weiss recognize him? Does he care? Does it matter at this point? Some townsman. A customer, certainly. At this point does it matter?

"'Where are you going?' And the second man, who held a torch, passed the torch to the third and motions up at the conductor, and points up at Weiss's family, who are aboard the train, and motions the conductor to remove them from the train. And he does.

"The train starts to leave. Starts to pull out. The conductor, looking back, shakes his head and mounts the train.

"Weiss and his family standing on the empty plat-form. The train pulling out.

" 'Where did you think you're going?'

" 'Sir,' Weiss says. "Sir . . . the signs said that the Jews . . . the *Jews* were to leave the town. . . .'

The man came forward and stood inches from him. '*Lord*, Mr. Weiss,' he said, 'not *you*. You're *our* Jew. . . .'"

The room erupted in laughter. The one cousin barked. Frank's wife slapped her thighs and looked at her sister Mayra, who was already removing her handkerchief and screwing up her face for tears. Frank shook his head and chuckled. Morris looked at him.

" . . . *our* Jew," Morris said, and shook his head, and nodded to the girl in the kitchen to say, "Yes. Now." And she came forward with the Passover tray.

The Seder plate

There was the fellow with the gun—an old matchlock, or wheel lock, misdrawn, for what would the Jews know about guns: nothing but to look away.

Nonetheless, there he was, pictured on the plate, around him, in Hebrew, the words *Matzoh, Maror, Karpas,* the ritual foods of the Passover seder, and, by each word, a small depression in the plate. And in the center, once again, the chap, as he thought of him, holding his rifle.

"What a medieval scene," he thought. "Wouldn't one expect a man in that attire to hold a crossbow . . . ?" For the chap wore a jerkin and what seemed to be a conical fur hat. He was caught in a resolute, misdrawn attempt to depict stealth, and there, beyond him, looking back, was the rabbit.

"Even I," Frank said to the man from New York, "even I, in my ignorance and sloth, know that it cannot be 'kosher' for a Jew to hunt."

He pronounced the word "kosher" gingerly, as if to say, I don't disclaim that I have heard it, but I do not wish to say it freely, as to arrogate it to myself on the mere precedent of blood.

I don't mean to disclaim it, but neither do I, for good or ill, wish to suggest a greater than accidental liaison between myself and that tradition.

"This is a very rare piece, I believe," the other man said, "and I'll explain it to you. You are most correct to state it is non-kosher—for we are enjoined against the shedding of blood other than quickly, painlessly, with respect, and by a man trained ritually and practically to ensure his competence, if I may. So, you are correct. That hunting is not kosher."

"Nor the hare," Morris said.

"The hare, no," the man from New York said, "although the rabbit is."

"What is the difference," Frank said, "between the rabbit and the hare?"

The man from New York began his response, and Frank thought, "I hate myself. Who am I trying to impress, or what accomplish, by that 'Jewish' flight of interrogation? God forgive me. No. And what do *I* care . . . ?"

". . . while the *hare*," the man continued, "is another species. Beyond that I cannot say."

"Which brings up," Morris said, "the *rationality* of the proscription."

"Yes, it might," the other man said. "Yes. It might."

There was a pause.

". . . the hare," Frank said.

". . . and there was a discussion," the New York man said, "at one time, about various animals. The various animals. Why fish, for example, should be parve, or 'neutral,' if you will, while chickens should be classed as flesh."

"I find this ludicrous," Frank thought. "Why do I pretend?"

". . . and the Rabbis," the man said, "in the Talmud, discoursed on the goose, as there had been an *observation*, at one point, by travelers to some distant land, of geese, it was said, *nesting in trees,* and so they undertook to discuss if the *goose* could be classed as a fruit." The man smiled slightly.

"Distant from where?" Frank said.

"Distant from where . . . ?" The man sought to connect the question to the discussion. Then he nodded. "Babylon. Palestine, it would be, as it is in the Talmud, that the travelers would have been distant from. Which is in the present day Mesopotamia and in that day was Babylon, and in that year, where would they have traveled to," he mused, "to see a goose in trees?"

"I loathe this man," Frank thought.

"I hate the whole tradition. An amusement of

slaves—calls itself philosophy. They might as well have chosen the advert on a pack of cigarettes and studied *it* four thousand years." He looked down. "'Costliest and most rare of tobaccos. Custom blended, selected, and cured for your smoking delight—a cigarette of distinction.'

"How many times could we find the letter *c* in here?" he questioned himself. "And what might that reveal to us of the workings of the world?"

"This idiot country," he thought.

"Though, on the other hand, what *might* it mean that the letter *c* . . ."

". . . the rules of . . . that land from which they came," the New York man droned on.

". . . and how many times, in the course of the day, do we jerk, if I may, convulsively, and call it 'reason'?" Frank thought.

"But to give up hunting?" Morris said. "That is steep."

The other man shrugged.

"All right, then," Morris said. "Why is the fellow on the plate permitted?"

The other raised one finger. Frank was filled with disgust.

"Like a cartoon I saw," he thought. "Judge on the bench. Old Jew in the dock. Judge says, 'If you were so innocent, why did you not explain yourself to the arresting officer?' Old Jew shrugs. 'I was *hendcufft*.'"

"Yahknehaz," the visitor said. "Y equals (Section K), which adds up to the *order*—in Hebrew, the *seder*—of the Ritual Meal.

"Yahknehaz. I put it to you, a German speaker, does it not resemble *Jagd den Hase*—the Hunting of the Hare? It does, I say. It does.

And I say it is ingenious to translate the mnemonic not *once but twice*—don't you think? Who could forget it?" He turned to address the table.

"And I *assure* you," he said, "having heard it once, you will never forget it till the day you die." He raised his finger. "And that was the most excellent genius of the Rabbis."

Discussion of the Mortara case

Life at the lake, of course, was easier.

It was, in its own particular way, more formal than the life in town. There was more of what he had come to think of as "social intercourse," which differed completely from the urban "visiting."

Most nights of the week the wives would sit out on one another's verandas, or gather at the hotel porch. And Saturday night—Sunday was "Family Night," sacrosanct to the reunion with the Husband up from Town—Saturday night and Sunday afternoons were given to the round of formal "Stoppings By," a round of dinners, breakfasts, parties, and teas offered and returned.

He loved the smell of breakfasts. The clean reek of

coffee, as if it went direct to his bowels. That's how it felt
to him, an excitement. Sunday morning, rested, a day free
of work, rising late.

The road was still—the dirt road up from the lake.
The townspeople were all at church, while he slept late
and woke to the feeling of entitlement.

What dearer sound than one's own wife moving care-
fully, to protect one's sleep, one's late sleep—what
greater endorsement?

"They may say what they like, Morris," he said, "but
the *Mortrara* boy, the matter of the *boy* is not a matter of
state. Not," he said, stilling correction, "*not* that I would
not have it so. I *would*. But what state, what . . ." He
spread the country honey on his toast and thrilled to the
sound of his own voice, holding forth. So like a man.
"So like a man," Frank thought. "Assured—*beyond* assured. *Didactic*, yes, I'm proud to say it. And why not? At
my own table, in front of my friends—who are *guests*. Yes.
And I speak without apology. It may be truth itself, it
may be *trash*, yes, though I do not think it is, but it may
be . . . it cannot be *both*, but . . ." His thoughts were interrupted as he came to "my due and prerogative" and was
about to proceed toward "the greater benefits of the
Leader, in this case, the Father, and the Family Gather-
ing, ruled or commanded or led by a Central Figure . . ."

"Where, then, *might* be the other possibility?" Morris
said.

"More toast"? his wife said.

"Yes," Frank thought. "I have my place, and she has hers. Our *happiness* comes from the limits we impose, both on each other and on ourselves. Our . . ."

Ruthie brought the platter in, and, as he did every week, he appreciated the old green platter and thought of it as "country crockery."

"So refreshing," he thought.

". . . if you would do it at the *factory*," Morris said.

"Do what?"

"What? Do what?" Morris said. "Do *what?*" And he looked across the table at his sister, to gather support.

"If I would . . . Yes, yes, yes," Frank said. "Yes. 'Act in' . . . well, *Morris. Morris.* Each of us has . . . don't we? Each . . . wait a moment . . ."

"How I love these discussions," he thought. "And after breakfast I will have a nap.

"Was ever a man in such a happy position as this? The coffee? The friends? The breeze from the lake, the breakfast? No. A man could live all the years allocated to the earth and not see a more lovely morning."

Soon they'd hear the boats, and the sound of their neighbors, returning from church, the rumble of the cars, and the quiet walk of the horses, and the voices of townspeople, talking low.

They were back, of course, on the rear veranda of the cabin. On the lake side—why should they not be?

"That's where the breeze is," Frank thought. "That is where the breeze is. And a man who works all week can stand a day of simple pleasure, away from the mass, the trouble, and the maintenance of the administration. Away from the inadequate strength of the last three shipments of cedar . . . now you've thought of it," he thought. And, through it all, heard himself speaking.

". . . government of Spain, a *sovereign* body. But as they . . . wait: Morris. Wait a moment. Morris . . ."

He sat, brooding over the indulgence due him, and deprived him, in the termination of his speech. He waited. Morris subsided.

"*Did,* I say. *Did* 'as they thought right.'" There was a momentary pause.

"Subsequent *events* . . . ," he continued, and raised his hand to still his friend, who bore the look of one practiced upon. "Well, if he wanted to speak, he should have *spoken,*" Frank thought, and continued.

All the while he was conscious of their position on the back porch, hidden from the road.

"No, we have the right to be here," he thought. "We are not 'screened' from them, for this is where the porch was built; and how could they take umbrage that we've not gone to church? We are not *sequestering* ourselves, for, surely, they can smell our breakfast, and that's the *end* to it."

"Well," Morris said, "I'm going to tell you something: They took that child, and the child's *gone.* How do you *deal* with it? You *deal* with it. How you deal with it, that's the meaning of philosophy. Fellow says, 'Meaning of philosophy,' you have to make your *own.* Now, generations: 'How many angels dance on the head of a pin?' One man comes along: 'How big is an angel?' Ah. This is a new philosophy. Ages go past. 'Aha. Aha,' so on. New man says, 'How big is the *pin?*' Mm?" He paused. ". . . hailed as a visionary."

Thoughts about advertising. "Wells Fargo Never Forgets"

'Wells Fargo Never Forgets.' "Well, that's a slogan, and all you need to know about that company. How could you forget it? And who would want to transgress them? To be outside the law?"

"What does it mean to be outside the law?" Frank thought. "Might one not take extraordinary pleasure from it? What must it be to loose the constrictions of the daily life—to be bound only by those one chose to observe, all this offset by just one thing: that one was hunted.

"If I could excise the *conscience*," he thought, "all that would be left would be the fear—no, it need not be fear—no, the 'fact.' The 'fact' of being hunted. Like the dog.

"That would be my life."

The dog had been coming to the porch of the hotel, nights.

Some said it was a wolf; some said a coyote; but both terms signified only a wild canine, and what was the difference, he thought, between the terms and the dog, who lay there dead?

Nothing at all.

The dog's domestication was an illusion. An illusion. He was as much a beast as the coyote or the wolf. There was nothing that he would not do—nothing he had not done.

So, what did it avail to think of him as a "dog"?

If he would come, as he came, night after night, and steal; if he would kill, as he had killed, the smaller animals around the hotel; if he would stand and, cornered, attack, as he had done, when trapped in the barn?

And now he lay shotgunned, dead, in the kitchen yard, nothing about him domestic.

He was wild. He had lived and died wild, and the rest was an illusion. Where he found it comfortable, necessary, where he found it convenient, or through lack of choice, he had lived in a house, and took scraps and obeyed masters who called it love.

When he turned from them, when he escaped, when he left, the world was his for the one price: to accept being hunted.

"Could I have as little conscience as the dog?" he asked.

"And now, you see, he traded A for B," Morris said.

"And there you have it?"

Morris walked through the dooryard with Frank. The women sat on the veranda.

"What do they talk of?" Frank wondered. "And why has Morris seen fit to comment on the dog? Yes, to assert his superiority."

And now the dog was dead, and Morris was saying that, as the dog should have known, his was a losing battle, and that that not given in love would be redressed in blood.

Was that true? That one's only choice was to obey or die?

"He would have died in any case," Frank said.

"I don't get you," Morris said.

"Well," Frank said, "it's not deep." They watched the dog lifted up with a shovel.

A large black man was called out of the kitchen. He came wiping his hands on a filthy apron. Morris and Frank walked away

He saw the groundsman gesturing to the dog, and the black man bobbing his head. He was handed a large coal shovel.

He scooped the dog into it. As Frank looked back, he saw the man with the shovel walking toward the margin of the woods.

"No. That's the wrong tool for the job," he thought, "if he intends to bury him."

Morris began to speak. "Yeaauh," he said. "Abrams's expanding."

"*Is* he?" Frank said.

Morris nodded. "Boston. Providence. Philadelphia."

"I hope he does well."

"Well, if he does well we do well," Morris said.

"That follow?"

"I think it does. To the extent that we are willing to go up against him."

"What does Jack say?"

"Haven't talked to Jack," Morris said. "But I intend to. Next time I . . . " He stopped to light his cigar. He motioned "wait a moment," and he bent over the cigar, shielding it, through habit, from a wind that did not exist that day.

"Y'ever notice?" he said between puffs. "Y'ever notice, cup the match *such* that, *were* it to catch on the book, it would flare up in your face?" He sighed. ". . . the matchbook.

"And as many times as I've remarked it, over the years, still I hold it in the selfsame way. Lighting the seegar."

"Well, you're human," Frank said.

"Ain't it the truth?"

They walked on, and Morris glanced at him, to say, "Now *what* the hell was I talking about?"

"Jack Fine," Frank said.

"Jack Fine. I said, 'The lifeblood of trade's competition.' 'I've always thought so,' Jack said. 'That being the case,' I said, "come you've never gone into New York?'"

Here Morris paused. He raised his eyebrows to show that the point of the story'd come.

"'Because,' Jack said, 'I go into a place, I want to know I am the smartest Jew there.'" Morris shook his head and grinned. Frank grinned.

"Yessir," Morris said, "lifeblood of trade." They walked on.

"Things the factory?" he said.

Frank looked to gauge the intent of the question. He saw nothing, and shrugged. "Up six percent, twenty-seven months."

". . . they say New York?" Morris said.

"Lloyd?"

"Mm."

Frank smiled. "Say very little."

"What have they turned, thankful?" Morris said.

The two men walked on.

"Wells Fargo Never Forgets," Frank thought. And he could not forget his thought of the shovel and the dog.

"Will I go to my grave," he thought, "with this uppermost in my mind, each moment of the day?"

In the courtroom, Frank heard the Judge drone on. And his eyes rested on the carved piece of denticulation in the cornice in the corner of the room. Soft, buttery wood, brown and, for some reason which he could not plumb but for which he was thankful, restful.

His gaze slipped, more and more now, to that point on the wall. And each time it did, he expected its calmative powers to've dissipated; and each time, upon discovery that they had not, he was grateful. But he would not stop thinking of the shovel and the dog.

"It was the wrong instrument," he thought again. "Either to carry the dog or to dig a hole—or, still, to dismember it. It was a *coal* shovel," he thought, "for God's sake. Did the man not *know* that?"

At the lake.
Morris does card tricks

He looked so serious.

"No," Frank thought, "I will not be taken in by it. No. It is all a ploy, capitalizing on my human instinct to respect the portentous. There is that in the ordering of his features which apes the solemn and momentous. So it is natural I would pay homage to it with still concentration.

"All the same, I know that it's a ploy and, all the while, his hands are busy while his eyes are still."

Frank lowered his eyes the minutest amount in, as he thought, a respectable counterfeit of attention or respect. And he saw the other man's hands were, as he had seen them last, folded, still, plump, one over the other, and both over the red deck of cards.

"But of course he has moved them," Frank thought. "He moved them in the instant in which he said "Now!'—when I lifted my eyes to his. I could observe him now forever and what difference would it make? The trick has been done."

Morris cleared his throat and Frank raised his eyes. He saw Morris's wife out of the corner of his eye—smiling, excited, and proud of the man holding the group's attention.

Behind them, by the door to the dining room, a black waiter stood, a tray of drinks on his palm. Frank saw the attitude of both respect and non-being in the man's demeanor. "I am here only when and as you desire me to be," it said.

And "Poor man," Frank thought. "It must grow tiring. To heft the tray, immobile on his palm, like that; though, perhaps, they grow used to it."

"I ask you now," Morris said.

"Perhaps it is just a question of balance," Frank thought.

". . . to tell me the name of the card you had chosen."

Frank looked back, behind him.

"The three of spades," Molly said. Morris nodded.

There were ten or twelve people on the porch, gathered before Morris, at his table. The men smoked cigars. The night wind took the smoke off the porch. Now and then the wind shifted, bringing back the scent of the trees and, once, the sound of paddles and high laughter on the lake.

"So still . . . ," Frank thought.

"Three of hearts. *Here* is the three of hearts!" Morris said.

He lifted his hands from the pack and fanned the cards over the table. They were facedown, save the one card, the three of hearts, which he drew from the pack, displayed, delighted, to the crowd, and threw, facedown, on the tabletop.

"No," Frank thought.

Morris looked at the faces on the porch. Two of the men coughed.

"Yes. What . . . what?" Morris said.

"I . . . Nothing," Molly said.

"What is it?"

"My card was the three of spades," Molly said. "Three of spades. Not the three of hearts."

Morris, then the rest, looked down at the solitary card, facedown, to the side of the spread pack.

". . . Your card was the three of spades . . . ," Morris said.

"*Oh*, yes," Frank thought, relieved. "Oh, yes. Now she will turn over the card, and it will have metamorphosed from the three of hearts to the three of spades. We will feel happy and relieved. Will we feel angry?

"What if it is *not* the case, and he has truly chosen the wrong card? How humiliating: to spend the hours

one must need in practice—practice to gain the approval
of the crowd—and then to disappoint them. How terrible: to have one's inner soul's longings revealed—'I burn
to tantalize you. To manipulate you, to control and delight you. To lead you in my ways and at my leisure'—
and then to fail. For what would obscure that personal
revelation? Nothing but success."

He heard the crowd draw in its breath, and break out
in laughter and exclamations.

For, of course, the card had transposed. And Morris
sat there, happy, confident, controlled, portraying the
least—but a discernible—measure of humility withal.

"Happy to please. Sorry to've taxed (if I did) your
patience. Sorry to've manipulated you. I hope that you
will find—as I found, for I did not act so without due
deliberation—that the misdirection was worth the result;
and that, finally, I have pleased." That is what he pro-
jected, sitting there.

Frank looked away and saw the waiter, who, similarly,
had reconfigured himself, and whose posture now an-
nounced that he knew the trick was concluded; that
though he did not wish to, and *would* not, appropriate
any of the group's enjoyment of the performance, he was
quite cognizant—to the limits of the intelligence autho-
rized to him—of its excellence. The waiter let the laughter and the semi-ironic applause begin to wane and, like
an actor playing the laugh, came forward with the drinks.

The evening passed.

Morris and Frank sat by the rail of the veranda.

"It is not cold," Frank thought, "but it will soon be cold."

There was a mist on the lake. The lights behind them in the hotel were dimmed. They heard the clatter, once, for an instant, of the last cleanings-up in the hotel kitchen, then stillness.

The breeze came through in one burst, across the porch. Then it was gone.

"Yeaauh," Morris said. He sucked at his teeth. "'Waal, Jedge,'" he said, repeating the punch line, "''if you was oncet a nigger on a Saady night, you'd never wan' to be a white man ev'again.'"

The backyard at night

He believed in it as if it were a religion.

For what was it but a mass of land, itself, an aspect of the imagination, really—for it stretched upon a piece of paper between here and there, and he said, "*Evidently, all of it must belong to the person who sees that cohesion, who sees that it lies between two oceans. And the person seeing that should own it, and that person is me.*"

What did it mean, to own it—to possess or to belong to a country?

He often thought of his house. And he delighted in his philosophical disquisitions on the nature of possession, and thought, "This is wealth. If I am unafraid to question my right in my home, then, surely, some merit should accrue to me, or, if not to me, to the act, an act of bravery. How *far would I permit the inquiry to go?* I do not know. But how many would have even dared raise the question?"

He rocked in his favorite chair, on the screened porch, as he looked out at the lawn, where Ruthie was picking some sort of grass or flower.

He'd had a mock fight with his wife: "We can never keep the girl out of the garden," he said; and she'd said, "Well, let her go."

He'd said, "She's a *house* servant, and what the hell is she doing out there when she should be working?"— both happy in the banter of no consequence about a minor foible of a family member.

One had to be the Chief to have the Chief's dilemma.

And it felt good to him. It felt good to smoke his cigar, and let the breeze take it out, through the screen porch. "The good ones," he thought. "When you stopped, you could hardly tell that there'd been smoking." They were his well-made, good Havanas. And why not? Did he not deserve them?

"Yes and no," he thought.

There were poor people in the world. There were those in pain and oppressed. And, yes, he had worked for the house, and still worked twelve hours a day, in a falling market; and who could say, God forbid, that the factory would not fold, or burn, or some . . .

"You see," he thought, "this is the *point* of it: There is

no certainty. None at all. None. We clothe ourselves in rectitude to hide our shame. Our shame of our lack of worth. It's all chance. All of it."

He faced the woman in the garden.

"That grass is clean," he thought. "And it's dry, and I'm sure she's not staining her dress. Lord. Look at her fat black ass."

He cleared his throat, and rearranged himself on the rocker.

He tipped the cigar ash into the smoking stand.

"You do not want to fidget with it, or tap it too often, as the ash *cools* the smoke—supposing always that you have a good cigar. But, on the other hand, why make a fetish of it?"

". . . as some do," another part of this dialogue ran, a small, interior portion of his mind speaking up. He chided it, gently, but with an authority. For was it not speaking to assess his response?

Could he not as easily respond, "You're damn right, and it's affectation"? Yes, he could, and then the inter-locutor would have got his instruction: "Yes. Yes. That is how we act, and that is the opinion we take. Of men who act that way." But he did not so respond. He chided that voice, saying, "Well, I'm sure each acts as he thinks fit"; and another voice, a supportive judge, so to speak, added, "If they *paid* for the cigar, what business is it of anyone in the world how they smoke it?"

But, in his colloquy, he silenced that voice, too, with

an understanding but gently dismissive nod, saying, "I know that you do not take my part to curry favor; and, in fact, I may share your distaste. But it is to *me* to dispense reprimands." He smiled to that voice, as if to say, "As if any were needed between us." He paused. "And I will not," he thought, "censure the other remark; I will not. For it is not mine to censure; but, as it may appear needful, only to 'correct,' which can only be done with kindness."

But, saying it all, he hated the men with their too-long cigar ash, for it invariably ended on their vest, or on the rug. There was a certain masculinity to it, but, given the eventual untidiness, he had to see it as a discourteous affectation.

And he hated the fact of the Big Cigar being identified with The Jew. If ever there were an instance of unfairness, he thought, that must be it. And were there not two sides to every issue?

He saw Ruthie begin to straighten up, one palm flat on the ground, as she pushed herself up from her knees, panting. "It must be difficult to carry that weight in this heat," he thought, and was pleased that he found no admixture of superiority in the thought.

"For, after all, I did not make myself thin. God made me thin," he thought. And, "What is better than this breeze?" as the breeze wrapped her cotton dress around the front of her thighs. "Black Nubian columns," he thought, "rounder than worked marble. Like stones washed in a tide pool."

She turned, carrying the little flowers, dwarfed in her left hand, and the breeze tricked the bottom of her hem into a peak.

She started up the stairs.

"I . . . I know, Mist' Frank, I know . . . ," she said, and smiled.

She opened the screen door and came onto the porch. She walked slowly past him, toward the door to the kitchen. ". . . I know," she said.

He felt that she felt his smile of indulgence, though he was not certain that it had broken through on his face. But he felt she knew it was there. He saw it in the quality or in the rhythm of her walk, in the timing of her opening of the door, in the way that she let it close. In a moment he would hear her in there, starting supper.

The heavy woolen jacket

But one is apt to spend a certain portion of one's income on appearances—perhaps "driven" to spend. This operation, he thought, is no different than the laborer's beer, or round of beers, at the saloon. No different at all. We need to *establish* ourselves, rich and poor. And the poor are always with us, as the Christians say. Is that not a quote from the Bible?

As he walked, he thought of the teaching of Christ: "It is easier for a camel to pass through the eye of the needle," and the struggle of the rich to understand this passage in a way not hurtful to themselves, he thought, "what a show that is."

"Yes, well, it is said, I have heard it said," he thought, "that it was said there was a gate in some old city, in Palestine, in Jerusalem, perhaps—for it is most probably just a story, and, as such, we'd just as well set it in the most prominent place . . . In Jerusalem, then," he thought, "there was a gate, or a turn, or a passage, called 'The Needle's Eye,' and so, and so, and so . . . "

He walked, and meditated on the folly of man.

"Deceive anyone but yourself," he thought.

"What is religion?"

Then there was the allied question of the shirt.

He wore it seldom, but thought of it often.

It hung on a hook by the back door. A heavy woolen jacket-shirt, which he thought of as a "rough" or "outdoor" garment.

It was gray, with light-green stripes at large intervals.

A shirt for working in the yard.

But he did not work in the yard. That work was done by Tom or Red, the friends ("common-law husbands," as he thought of them) of Ruthie.

He wore the shirt perhaps five times in the year, on the rare cool morning or evening when he'd choose to walk back into the yard to smoke his cigar. He'd take the metal chair from the group by the back door, on those occasions, and retreat the thirty-five yards to the live oak tree, and sit there and smoke, and there congratulate himself on what he felt was an almost bohemian behavior.

Such occasions were always preceded by an inner dialogue in which he would adopt two basically conservative positions and, in yet a third guise, or voice, as "moderator," bring them into a reasoned accord.

"Why should I not simply walk back into the air—clothed, in fact, 'however'—and there, unseen and unsuspected, enjoy my cigar? And if I am remarked, then, what then? Have I not seen men . . . "

Here he nodded, in deference to imaginary listeners who might, absent this obeisance, interpret the coming phrase, "of my class," as arrogant. He paused. ". . . men of my class," he continued, "in similar, surely, in undress *surpassing* my adoption, or, yes, or say "affectation" of the lumber jacket? Have I not seen such men, and that *frequently*, out 'in their yards'?"

Here the opposing voice suggested clothing designed for the lumber camp was best worn there. And so it went.

And here, usually, the voice of inanition informed him that he was walking to his study to smoke, and so he did, in the sanguine mood. Happy to be possessed of a liberality sufficient to allow contemplation of the free-spirited art of philosophy.

And on the rare times when he walked back to the live oak, that voice's companion spirit spoke, and praised him for conservatism grounded enough to function healthily and secure in spite of appearances.

He wore the shirt seldom, but it plagued him all year long.

For, in his mind, he'd promised it to Ruthie.

He and his wife regularly assembled their cast-off clothes and passed them to the maid.

So he'd long wanted to give the shirt to her, as he felt it mean to hoard an article he used so infrequently.

But when his wife assembled the used clothes—as she did once or twice a year—he hesitated before adding his shirt to the pile. He'd argue with himself and, finally, consign the hated shirt; and, as invariably, return to the pile later that day, to retrieve it and replace it on the hook by the back door.

His unspoken vow occurred to him with regularity sufficient to suggest, when he did think about it, that it was never out of his thoughts—that he, at any given time in his life, was involved in two simultaneous occupations: the matter of the moment, and his battle with self-loathing over his inability to honor his vow and dispose of the shirt.

"It stands for all I hate in myself," he thought.

"Another man would burn the cursed thing, and, so be done with it."

So it was with the other matter of the couch.

"We are plagued," he thought, "with possessions. Those who have them not yearn for them. Those who have them yearn, at once, for more and for their freedom from them.

"But there are those," he thought, "worse than I—for they are not even conscious of the mechanism. They, in short, live like poor, driven beasts."

The Confederate flag

Now the breeze took the water from the garden hose as the boy lifted it, the breeze took it, for one brief moment, into a roostertail in the air. Then the boy brought it down. What had moved him to lift the hose? "Exuberance, certainly," and, "What a miracle," Frank thought. "What a blessing the water was."

The flag, however, was heavier. The breeze moved it hardly at all. Of what material was it? Almost certainly a canvas. Not new. Weathered, how many years old? He could not remember when they'd first put it up. Had they hung it every year? Stars and Bars. The reds faded to a sort of purple. "Well, the sun will do that," he thought. And he thought back to the other flags.

"Rags, really. Battle ensigns. If," he thought, "that is indeed the correct style."

Battle flags, carried in the Confederate Memorial Day celebration.

"Old men, now. Old men. How could they not be? So proud. As the town was proud. And why should they not be?" It was good to have tradition. Who was he to say it was wrong?

Yes, slavery was wrong. But the War had been fought over more than slavery. If, in fact, it had been fought over slavery at all—was it only the Jews who had that earnest discussion? The rest of the world seemed to've accepted this received notion of History. Why should they not? They'd fashioned it, and moved on.

But the Jews, as the Jews said, the Jews would worry it to death, and love the sad irony of the Southern side.

There were the Jews, celebrating exodus from Egypt, and free to use the full play of their intellect to probe the causes, the cures, of the Institution.

"There was economic servitude," as Morris said, "as *severe* as bodily indenture. And the position of Southern merchants, in *thrall* to the North, unable to . . ."

Every year—it was a family joke—he would start his speech, and every year he was laughed to a stop, and he *would* stop, appreciating the affection in which he was held. But he would shrug, to say, "However, there is some merit in my case, which you may see someday," and someone would say, "Government intervention is damned meddling, unless we *need* them, when we call it Humanity," or some such, and they would play their ritual out every year. For it assured them that they were home.

And was that not the point of ritual? For what was going to be settled at the Seder table? At *any* family conclave? The point of worth was the liberty to discuss, and, beyond that, below that, the solidarity—the joy of being the same as everyone there, which joy was only underlined by their playing at differences.

The argument was their ritual. Others had their observances, he thought, which defined them, which assured them, for the savagery they feared was not in the world, as they thought, but in their minds. And who could grapple with that?

In the kitchen, behind him, were the sounds of supper being cleared away. The last sounds.

Who could grapple with it? he thought. A factory. Why? Workers. Why? The Wage System. Why? Slavery, freedom.

Across the way, the Confederate Flag hung in the heat. "It drapes down but is not defeated," he thought. "It hangs stiffly."

And he thought it hung too stiffly—that the material, fashioned for wear, did not allow the flag to loft: as he phrased it to himself, to "wave like a banner."

On his walk to work tomorrow he would see thousands of them. On the homes, in lapel pins, on cars, the thousand banners in the parade, certainly. And he wondered about the business of the flags. "For any business," he thought, "protected by sanctimony should prosper." He nodded.

"Flags . . . funerals . . ." He searched for a third example.

Behind him he heard Ruthie putting the last dishes away, and the clink of the latch of the pantry. Now she was done. Now he would hear her padding to the stairs out back, where she would sit and catch her breath.

Now his wife was upstairs. Sitting in bed. Reading. Now he should go to bed. Now he should lay his cigar down in the smoking stand to let it go out, and get up and go to bed.

There was work to do tomorrow. The problems of the world would keep. And what were they, finally, but a diversion? We could not know them, he thought. We spoke of them, if we knew it, simply as entertainment, he thought, and sighed, and smiled with affection at his gentle folly.

The new couch

At some point it had become important to him to have a new couch. He had first ignored and then pretended to ignore his wife's hints about redecorating.

When she raised the subject openly he had resisted and explained to her that the circumstances of their life were comfortable and correct, and, in fact, lavish if compared to the median state of man at any time, and at this particular time in any place that she might mention.

As he spoke on that first occasion, he both knew and did not know she would eventually prevail. As he became more comfortable with the duality, he explained it to himself in this way:

"Though she is wrong, it is fitting that there be certain aspects of life in which she can prevail.

"In most of married life she follows my command. Now equity and common sense—even were there no affection—suggest that I occasionally recognize her claims. How galling, in fact," he reflected, "to have no part in life in which one can prevail."

He reminded himself, then, to be gracious, and to find it in himself truly to ratify her claims, rather than merely to appear to do so.

"For does she not, by her lights, make these decisions (as she feels) for our mutual benefit? Yes," he thought. "Yes, she does—in no way unlike myself—in electing this or that improvement in favor of our mutual domestic life."

And so he told her she could redecorate, and was ashamed of his chagrin when she took his capitulation as a matter of course, and launched into a recital of plans which obviously had been not only thought out but well-nigh implemented long since.

"*This* is my task," he thought, "not to 'grant,' no, but to recognize that to grant is, in this, outside of my gift."

And yet he struggled to resist the simultaneous feelings of pride in his very humility and condescension in the residual conviction that his wife chose to find important the right to legislate regarding trivia.

"Yes. After all of it," he thought, and, "This is as it should be. She is just a woman."

But his thoughts of the changes to come worked on

him. And he sat on his leather chair, and looked at his couch, at the old comfortable couch where he'd lain so many evenings after work, which cradled him those many Saturday afternoons when he'd slept, his workweek done.

He looked across to the couch, and he saw not the couch but the couch-to-be. And he found he was impatient.

The old couch, the old room, looked to him passé. He found it important to have the new designs completed and installed, but he could not determine why he found it so.

"As I attempt to analyze it," he thought, "I recognize this (I must say) basic, and I could say, 'savage,' need to be accepted by the community."

Here he made a note on a leaf of his letterhead notepad.

The note read:

Advertising must appeal, as is its essential nature, to the fear that one is to be excluded. It must both *awaken* and *suggest how to allay* this fear.

The heading on the notepaper sheet read, "National Pencil Company. Atlanta, Georgia."

The voice of the prosecutor dwelt on that word each time he said it. "How lovely it is," Frank thought, "that people can communicate so. He does not *pause* so much as *inflect*, and he does not *inflect* so much as *signify*—in a way which, were we to reproduce and dissect his rhythm and pronunciation, would be absent. For science cannot discover it. It is a *spirit*," he thought. Frank heard the prosecutor drone on: ". . . that it is usurpation for a company to descend to the South and to call itself "National."

Frank smiled, in an experimental trial of the irony. "And that is what they're going to kill me for."

That Saturday

There was a heavy summer smell, and there was the question of the ink.

"You'd think," he thought, "that it would get into the house and cause mildew, but it is just this side of that; and if you paid attention, you would know it. In the smell. That it was laden and wet, but it stopped short of being harmful, if you had the courage to recognize that you knew it.

The humidity was not going to harm anything except your sense of order. And if you were required to pay for it, you'd pay for it later in the day, in the heat. "Well, now," he thought, "will that assuage your sense of fairness? For was there not a breeze in the world? Yes. There was, he thought, as he sat down to breakfast.

And they said the ribbons in the typewriting machines would last two or three months. But he wondered, as they seemed to last longer, if it was a function of the *humidity*.

"What is ink?" he thought. "Some substance which maintains semi-liquidity sufficient to allow its transfer, and then dries into a solid state.

"Some *dye*, in effect, of that description." And could it not be that the humidity of his city kept the ribbons moist, kept the ink moist, and could it not be that the insufficiency of the company's estimate reflected not the absence of ink at the end of two months but the desiccation of the ink and ribbon, and that *moistening* . . . ?

He nodded at Rose, as she sat. He tried to envision a remoistening of the typewriter ribbons. How would it take place? Could one wind and immerse them, and why was that image, he wondered, not as satisfying as the, granted, more elaborate scenario of unwinding the spool to its total length—whatever that might be?" ("What might that be," he thought, "a hundred yards? Hardly. Fifty? Twenty, more likely . . .")

"These are the musings," he thought, "of a content man."

"At twenty yards"—he smiled at the thought— "some might call me silly. *But* if the ribbons were strung building-to-building, in the rain—wouldn't that moisten them? Now, is that idiocy, or an elegant solution? Who can say?" he thought. "Who could say, who hadn't tried it? If, finally, if—*if* moisture was, in fact, the problem. And here I am, *already* surpassing their estimate by thirty percent.

"Are these the thoughts," he wondered, "of a miser?" And he answered himself, "No, no. I don't think so. I think that it's *business*, and it's all reducible to that; and if the care, and foresight, yes, and yes, and *dreaming*, isn't business, then I do not know what is.

"The man who invented the *wheel*. Think of that. *Think* of it. How many millennia of placing a free roller underneath a load. And people dreaming, dreaming, 'If I could dispense with carrying these rollers: but how?' and someone, probably, thought of fixing rollers underneath the load, to be axle and wheel at once. But the *genius*," he thought, "the *genius* . . . and must he not have shivered as he thought of it, not in triumph, but in fear. In *fear*: 'Can it work? How can it work? If it *could* work, would someone not have invented it before?'

"In *fear*, he must have had the insight, the notion, to *abstract* the roller into two 'wheels.' And must he not have thought: 'Why me?'

" . . . Why me?" He nodded.

"For, if he was right, then the rest of the tribe was wrong, and had been wrong for millennia—not to see the obvious.

"And then," he thought, "they could not see the *obvious*, and . . ."

The double-hinged door banged open, and Ruthie came in with the coffeepot.

"These are the thoughts of a happy man," he thought. "Have I tempted fate?" And: "Jesus Christ, this coffee smells good."

"Starting to turn hot already," he thought, as he left the house.

"Turn hot. Parade. Well, that's as it should be. Price for everything. Some mornings, in the damp, you feel it as a coming penance; some mornings as a reprieve."

Already the flags were flying. Up and down his street. Confederate Flags. He nodded as he walked past them.

"Everyone has a right," he thought. "Who is to say he's less misguided than his adversaries?" He thought: "*Any* of us. To believe in this or that? When, five years, ten years, our beliefs change that completely we wonder, 'What *can* I have meant . . . ?'

"And, of course, it's a religion. The State. Any state, perhaps; and a good thing, perhaps, at that.

"For how is it different from a company? It is not. It *is* a company. A Group of Men. Organized under a set of Principles which, perhaps they may think—but they are in error—which will cover all contingencies.

"Now: what do they do when situations arise outside

the scope of the Precepts upon which the Concern was founded?"

"Good morning, Mrs. Breen," he said.

"Good morning, Mr. Frank. Goin' to work?"

"Yes. Off to work. Off to the office."

"Don't miss the parade," she said.

"Oh, no. I wouldn't miss it, I," he said. "You know, I *see* it—I can *see* it from my fifth-floor windows."

"You *can't*. In the fact'ry?"

"Yes, I can." He smiled. A little piece of Pear Street. "Yes, indeed, I can."

"Hmm," she said, wagging her head slightly, as to say, "What do you know . . ."

They stopped there for a moment, and she sighed. "Going to be warmish," she said.

"Well, I should say so. I'd say it's going to be quite warm."

He tipped his hat and continued down the street.

The Coffee Corner

The two men sat in the Coffee Corner, with their hats pushed back on their heads.

"'Waal, if they don't, I will,' many would say. And I'm not sure I would, but I can't discount it. In the right circumstances. An' it's one thing come acrost a thing, you follow: see a fellow in the act, and *stop* him . . ." They nodded.

"There in the *heat*, eh . . . ?"

". . . Yeaauh," they said, and nodded.

". . . in the *heat*. Or even after. Look: I can't discount it. A man need to see some justice done. 'Ven *after*. I can see that. Take out your pistol, *bam*. A man's got feeling. 'N' I want to *tell* you something." He hitched his chair closer to the counter.

"All the laws in the world, and all the religion, to one end: to try to *legislate* . . ."

". . . uh huh," they said.

". . . keep these feelings in check. Well. Fine. You mizewell . . . " He shrugged, and his hand searched the air for the perfect comparison, the cigarette in the hand like a part of it, his fingers like yellow morocco leather, stained by nicotine, the nails huge and cracked. " . . . you mizewell . . ."

". . . water in a sieve," a friend said.

He pointed his finger at the friend, to say, "You have hit it exactly."

"All the laws in the world," he continued, "all the laws in the world, Jesus Christ himself, in the heat of a *blood* passion . . .

"Because, boys, *wait* a second," he said. "Because what we are talking about here is Human Nature. And you tell me that that's not a mystery? And self-control? How many, you think, 's in there armed? Any meetin'? Any . . ."

The others murmured.

". . . mm?"

"That's right," a friend said.

". . . 'n' you tell me that's not an instance?"

". . . self-control . . ."

". . . waal, I don't know it's self-*control* . . ."

"What is it, then?"

". . . self-"

" . . . what?"

"Waal, I'm *telling* you, you'd listen to me," the man said, as the other men at the counter waited, as at a long-watched and long-appreciated comedy turn.

"I think that it is *equally* a desire. Mm? To be *part of a group.* Wait: not to *violate* . . ."

". . . that's right," the other man said.

". . . to . . . hmm? To put the *interests* of the group *before* himself."

". . . before who?"

"That man with a gun. Mm? That man, as you said, who's out there, who, in the interests of his *group,* to which he belongs—or, or, wait a second, to the urge not to be ostracized, out *of* the group, that's all right—refrains from the action, eh, which would *ostracize* him. Mm? That's self-control. Or not, as you may choose to put it. I don't know what it is. You finish your coffee you c'n tell me."

Frank walked by the Coffee Corner, and he looked in at the men.

The watch

Could it be the desire for the watch which had doomed him?

As he walked down Hazel Street he wanted to turn down Rutherford.

"No," he said. "I can choose or avoid any route that I wish; and my *detour*, if one can call it that, is nothing more than an *alternative*. An alternative of no greater length than the original or—"More direct," his mind supplied. "*Not* more direct," he responded. "Yes. Perhaps more direct. Perhaps. Though I do not stipulate it, but add that the desirability of a route, in this case, can be judged according to differing criteria: the *length* of a route; its . . . its . . ."

"Well, yes," another portion of his mind said. "Yes, We can allow it."

"Its . . ." he thought, and bowed slightly, as in thanks for the concession, "its *beauty* . . ." That was the word allowed him. He nodded.

A cardinal fluttered in the corner of his eye. He turned to see it, expecting to find it gone. But, no, there it was, in the tree on Walnut Street. And he walked and found he was on Main Street and had not, after all, turned down Rutherford, and he was on Main Street, walking as he had vowed not to do, and there he was in front of Winford's, and there was the watch.

"What garbage is man," he thought.

"What a swine I am—although mischance and not wilfulness took me here. Forgetfulness," he thought, "or a preoccupation took me here. Although their existence could be accounted as weakness."

But there was the watch. It sat in its purple-blue velvet box in the window. The inside lid was lined in silk, imprinted in gold with the letters "Breguet, Paris," and, beneath that, in small block letters, "For Winford's, Atlanta."

It was a full hunter. A slim pocket watch in rose gold. The case was covered front and back with small diamond cross-hatchings, which, Mr. Winford had told him, were known as "diapering."

"Breguet," Winford had said. "Napoleon carried a Breguet watch at Waterloo." He paused. "And so did Wellington."

"That a fact?" Frank had said.

On two days he had gone in, and Winford had displayed the watch: the elegance of the lines, the precision of the movement, the repeater function, which chimed the hour, the quarter, and the odd minute when one pressed the small gold stud.

Frank had never seen a repeater watch up close before; and when Winford caused it to work, Frank's reaction, as he phrased it to himself, was "like a savage on seeing an airplane."

The jeweler pressed the stud, and the watch, in a musical, but by no means effete, tone chimed ten, and then, in a higher tone, one-two-three; and after a pause, on the same note, in quicker rhythm, one-two-three-four-five.

"Ten-fifty," Winford said. And Frank felt he had to check to see if his mouth hung open.

"Full hunter. Gold repeater," Winford said. "Breguet, Paris. Lucky to get it. Doubt if ten come into the country this year."

Frank, looking at the watch, felt that his whole character was revealed. "I stand before that man," he thought, "unmasked as a grasping, an idolatrous swine."

For, when the watch chimed ten-fifty, and Winford interpreted the notes, did not Frank extract his perfectly good, his in fact superb, Illinois from his vest pocket? Did it not read ten-fifty, and was it not likely and was he not old enough to know it likely that, had he purchased the new watch, he would find it inferior to the one he carried?

"A man with one watch knows the time," he'd quoted to Winford. "A man with two watches is never sure."

"No, I'd not heard that one before," Winford said. He waited an amount of time to show respect for Frank's right of refusal, but not so long as to indicate he thought the customer less than decisive. He took the watch and returned it to the box, and the box to the window, and Frank left the store.

The second time he came, he felt fully within his rights.

It was not excessive to examine at length and on more than one occasion such an important—not to say costly—object.

For was that not the point? How could one consider spending three hundred dollars on a watch?

Although it was a rarity. Although, as Winford delicately observed, it would bid fair to increase in value, although it was a gift or recompense other successful men awarded themselves in the form of the automobile, the boat, the second home, the Sporting expedition.

Finally, "Finally," he said to himself, "finally, it was wrong."

It was wrong for him to own more than one watch. For him to spend that money on that watch. It was wrong. How did he know?

He did not know how he knew. But it was wrong.

Could one construct and defend the opposing argument?

Yes. And have it prevail—with any adversary but oneself. For the unconquerable fact—and he knew it to be a fact—was it was wrong: he knew it to be wrong. And he shrugged—less against this self-denial of the watch than at this new self-knowledge: that there was a force in the world superior to the individual, and that that force regulated action in those to whom it appealed.

He could not wish it away.

And here he was, swine that he was, once again on the sidewalk outside Winford's. He saw the jeweler in the store, talking to a salesgirl. And the man looked up and nodded at him.

"Son of a bitch," Frank thought. "Does he mean to assert he does not *care* if I buy the watch? Does he think I do not know his courtesy *point by point* is nothing other than the attempt to induce me to purchase it?"

Winford came out of the store, shielding his eyes against the morning glare.

"Can he mean to accost me," Frank thought, "with some comment either about or—the more effective (so he might think)—*not* about the watch? What other reason or what pretext might he have to come out here?"

Winford was turning the placard in the door from "Open" to "Closed."

"Going downtown, Mr. Frank?" he said.

"Yes. Down to work. Nice morning."

". . . Working today?"

"Yes. Odds and ends. You're closing?"

"Half-day. M'morial day. Half-day. Might as well."

". . . Mm?"

". . . No business. Not to speak of."

"Everyone downtown, eh?"

"I would think so." He paused. "Down the parade."

As they stood nodding for a moment, they heard the faint sounds of a band, far away, and particularly of several horns warming up.

". . . Yeessssss . . . ," Winford said.

"Wealllup," Frank said. He caught himself as he started to reach for the watch in his vest. "*No,*" he thought. He hoped that Winford had not seen what could be interpreted as a gesture on his part to open dialogue about a watch. But Winford was already turned away, and speaking to the shopgirl, who passed between him and the half-closed door.

"'Bye, Mr. Winford."

"Good day, Sal," he said.

"Yes," Winford said. "You have a good day, Mr. Frank."

Frank nodded and walked on. He heard the sound of the man stepping back into his shop, and the sound of the heavy shade being drawn down.

"That's good," Frank thought. "That's needful to keep the sun off the carpet. Bleach it out quick as you please." He walked on.

"What a fool I am," he thought.

The factory

The fan fluttered the bookmark off his desk. He watched the bookmark, flat, climbing, and falling, as the fan swiveled to the other corner of the room.

As it returned, the bookmark fluttered again, and rose, as if to fly. Then it fell back.

Rogerson's Stationery. 231 Main, Atlanta. Telephone: Maple 231.

Everything for your Office Needs.

And then the fan came back again.

"What would it take," Frank thought, "to flip it over? What's printed on the reverse? I should know it. It *lists*, as I remember," he thought, "various services, various goods, which they provide. Quite handy. Simple but true. One *uses* a bookmark. If that bookmark advertises a concern, we think of it each time we see the book-mark.

"Each time," he thought, "the fan returns in much the same way—making the allowance for the minute but inevitable wear inside the machine; making allowance, again, for the small but, I am sure, measurable shift of the fan along the desk—although it does seem fixed. Though the foam padding on its base no doubt reduces to near nil its motion. Even so," he thought, "even so. Even so. If I left for a period of months, on my return would I not see the fan had shifted, slightly? If I had marked its position out, on my departure, would I not see, upon my return, that change? And if I *could* not measure it, would not an absence of *years . . .*" He cast his mind ahead, to a return to his office in decades, in centuries, in aeons, until a time when he would not be disappointed to find the fan yet unmoved.

"For it *must* move," he thought.

"And if it moves, yes, even after the passage of *centuries*, if the passage of time shows it to have moved, then it must have been in motion all the time. For a measurable jump is nothing save the aggregate of these shifts we are incompetent to perceive.

"And if the *fan* moves, then the bookmark must move. As I watch it, it does not move; it flutters and falls in what seems to me to be the same space. And, of course"—he shook his head sadly—"the situation will not and cannot endure as a laboratory experiment." He shook his head and took a cigar from his humidor and lit it briskly, looking down at the bookmark, as at a recalcitrant and willful specimen of organism.

"For change is inevitable," he thought.

"This office cannot endure. Civilizations *themselves* are found, buried under aeons of dust—though I do not conceive how sufficient time could pass, even over a length of time, granted, which I must find unimaginable, to obscure a fifteen-story building . . ."

He consigned this thought—the question of the verity of the proposition that complete civilizations could be buried in dust—to that quality of things which both were and were not true.

"How can we hope to know," he thought, "if these things occur? If, in the very nature of the thing, we cannot live to see their outcome?

"*Nor,*" he thought, rising forcefully to what he felt was clearly the true burden of the argument, "nor can we control all the variables.

"Not only can we not suppose to live for that amount of time, but I am impotent even to control the entrance and egress to and from my office. Even should I say, '*Miss Scholz,* I wish no one to enter—even to clean— for some time.'" He nodded, meaning: "a reasonable request."

"'. . . Neither to disconnect the fan. I wish it to run.'"

He smiled ruefully.

"Is there not, as we know, *always* that reason, either ignorant, good-, or ill-willed, to 'interpret' my instructions?"

The bookmark skittered across the desk. He looked for the cause, and found it in the snap of the shade—in the one burst of breeze through the window.

"No, no, all things must end," he thought. He took the bookmark and placed it at the open page in the ledger—the left-hand entry completed. Date: Saturday, April 24, 1915. He dipped his pen and added the date of the next business day, Monday, April 26, at the top of the right-hand page. He blotted it and closed the ledger. He pushed it to one side of the desk, then brought it back and opened it again, and turned the bookmark to read: "Printing and binding, typist services, paper, ink, full ledger and bookkeeping services . . ."

He nodded and replaced the bookmark, and closed the book.

The shade snapped again. "Starched sound," he thought. "Not a thing in the world wrong with that."

He walked to the window and looked down. The heat smelled, he thought, clean, from the fifth floor.

"'S hot to walk up, but clean at this height," he thought.

The paper clip

"But I could throw the paper clip away," he thought. Why should I hesitate to save it? And is this a function of advertising; and, if so, of what is advertising a function?

"For in what way is the paper clip on the letter I've received different from those in the box? Now," he thought, "now: if I were the sort of man, or, barring and not going to that length, if I possessed," he thought, "the *habit*"—he grinned—"of keeping the paper clips in the box in which they arrived—and why should I not, as it's an attractive box (and, finally, the question is one of *utility*, which is to say, a man's self-understanding of the world)—

"Many would keep them in the box in which they came; and it is, arguably, defensibly (as if I required a defense) more prudent to do so. But, on the other hand, the box, over time, will wear down through my opening and closing it. And I assert—as if there were need of an assertion, and as if mere preference or *habit* (as I said before)—absent a conscious preference—did not suffice—

"If I kept, as I say, the paper clips in the cardboard box, would it not, arguably, conduce more toward the *waste* of those clips I receive on the mail I receive?

"Would it not, perhaps minimally but nevertheless, conduce to their waste, as one would then be less inclined to remove and to put them into a box full of—well, get on with it [he thought]—those which they did not match?"

And here he relaxed; his inchoate, unacknowledged thought: "There, I've said it."

"How far we come from ourselves," he thought.

"In the purchase of a receptacle for the clips I supply the impetus for their reuse. I decrease waste. I increase the beauty of my desk—but in truth, in all truth and finally, I do it, all of it, because I want to, and for no reason other or apart from that. And I may say 'it suits me,' or, 'it suits my sense of fitness', or, 'I find it pleasant,' or I may retreat one step and refer to the utility—for which I care not at all; not at all; not one jot—of the box.

"For, yes, small habits are the foundations of large; and, yes, in a business with small margin the least savings not only aggregate but . . . but, one may say, the least savings are the *only* savings. What *is* there but the 'least savings'?

"How often do we move house, purchase new machinery, or strike new contracts with our suppliers or with our help?

"No. No. Those things which we call 'small' and those which we call 'large' are, if we—"

Here he was interrupted, as the girl came in.

She showed him her time card, and he took the black box out and paid her, and she went away.

"Now," he thought, "I have bent the paper clip into a shape. I did it semi-consciously, because, I assume, the action itself was pleasing. And, having begun, I continued.

"Now it is useless. I have fashioned it into nothing at all."

"You went," the prosecutor said.

"You went," he said, "you went down to the basement. *Following* the girl, you called to her to turn, on some excuse—no doubt having to do with her *pay*. For she had *rebuffed* you—had she not? She had *rebuffed* you—how many times? And she had learned to *shun* you. And yet you called out, and she turned. And you pushed her down the stairs." He paused. "And ravaged her." He paused again, and shook his head, slowly. He cleared his throat. "And ravaged her. And beat her. And you took her life."

Frank looked up at the corner of the room.

The power of advertising

He sat at his desk and looked down at the bag.

"Now, that," he thought, "is good advertising.

"You see that and you remember it. You don't forget something like that . . . the look of it, nor the message of it. For it is"—he thought of the word and wondered if it, in fact, existed, and, in the spirit of the object which he examined, elected boldly to employ it whether or no.

"It is proclamative," he thought. "Proclamatory. Unabashed, and I like it like that."

On the desk was an old bank bag of heavy burlap. Ten by fifteen inches, the corners reinforced with coarse, heavy leather.

It closed with a drawstring sewn through the short end, and the drawstring ends drawn through a toggle the size of a poker chip. When the bag filled, the toggle would be pushed up against the bag, the string would be knotted tight up against it, and the knot sealed with wax. The toggle was of ocher gutta-percha. Pressed into it was the image of a hanged man and the motto "Wells Fargo Never Forgets."

"I would believe it," he thought. "I would believe it; and, were I of a criminal bent, I would choose to exercise it upon some other concern. *That* is the power of advertising. To induce or persuade to forgo the process of deliberation and suggest there is a higher method of arriving at a solution—a more immediate and a better method. That is the power of advertising."

The end of the day

And now his day was done. And it was quiet. The parade had ended, and he was alone.

It occurred to him that, in the office, on those days when he was alone, when he did his correspondence himself, he would always tear, from the sheet, the exact number of stamps he required.

Alone, on a Sunday, or on a Saturday afternoon, having completed his letters, having addressed them and sealed the envelopes, he would turn to the drawer and remove the buff folder which held the sheets of stamps. He would tear a crenellated block of stamps from the sheet—up and across, up and across—and when he turned his attention to paste them on the mail, whether he'd done five or ten or forty letters, he would find he had torn off that exact number of stamps.

It pleased him. And then he would denigrate both his achievement and his pleasure, thinking, "This is not, as I would enjoy it, a sign of 'election,' no; but merely the logical expression of a skill practiced so many times as to've become automatic.

"It would be remarkable," he thought, "if, on the other hand, I were *not* able, unconsciously, to approximate the number of stamps.

"Yes, yes. Yes, but," a small voice said, "you've not approximated it. You have hit it exactly. As you do each time you perform the task." It was this thought that nagged him, each time he approached the moment in the day when he would take out the buff folder.

"I know I can do it," he thought, "if and as long as I am 'unconscious' of it. *And* I know I can do it even conscious of the process; but I do not know if, conscious of the process *and* conscious of my pleasure—in that way which only can be vanity, which only can be idolatry (for have I not said that I do not 'approximate' but *exactly fulfill* the correct number? do I not discount my ability as quite normal and, at the same time, reserve the right to feel it . . . to feel it . . ." Here a small descant in his mind added the words with which he was loath to comfort himself: "a sign of election". . .) "I do not know if in *that* case I can do it."

Sometimes he would will the number of stamps *not* to correspond with the number of envelopes. Infrequently this would occur.

Then again, he would berate himself for the pleasure he felt.

"As if," he thought, "I now reward myself for contriving not merely achievement but randomness."

Finally, the meaning of the ceremony, he thought, was this: It came at the end of a perfect time.

After a Saturday afternoon or a Sunday alone, or virtually alone, inside his office, in the factory—able to catch up on the elusive ends of the business, able to put his house in order. Somewhat at his leisure. Like a chef, he thought, perhaps: after the banquet. Ordering his kitchen.

He cherished his time alone in the office. He felt it was a reward, a Sabbath, even though he was at work.

He felt a sort of pleasant omnipotence in doing his own correspondence. In it he found leisure to contemplate and power to express.

In it he stemmed the torrent of business and diverted it and made it run to a purpose and to his pace. And it all ran though him.

And if he chose to rest, to look out of his window, to smoke a cigar, to lie down on the couch and smoke a cigar into the heat, his coat on a hanger in the press . . .

If he rested the back of his shoes, above the heels, on the arm of the couch, his head low, the ashtray next to him, close by his left hand, down on the rug, his mind drifting to thoughts of that girl, of any girl, of girls like those in the mural in the club: high breasts, small boyish hips, no waist which could not be encompassed by his hands . . . And once he woke with a start, in a fantasy of fire, his back wet with the sweat of a too-deep summer nap.

Well, then, the thing for that, as he well knew, the universal tonic, was iced coffee. And thank God for someone to run for it.

What could be better than iced coffee, with just the merest drop of cream? And how he pitied those "unweaned," as he thought of it, who took it one part coffee to two parts milk.

Iced coffee. Just a drop of cream. No sugar, thank you, to exacerbate the heat of the day; a wet towel to wipe his neck, and then a dry one. The handkerchief from the side pocket folded in under the shirt collar.

Then the coffee would come, and then he would have a cigarette, back at his desk, his correspondence almost done.

It was a reward to order it into the stacks, the one of envelopes, the other of letters, then to reduce the two to one.

One stack of correspondence, waiting for the stamps.

And then the coda of the stamps. For the brief, anxious, but enjoyable byplay was just a leave-taking, was it not? Yes, he thought, it was. After which he would have to go home.

The trial

He had heard the Yiddish curse "May you be involved in a lawsuit when you're right." And now he understood it.

He saw that the wrong side could and would allege anything, unbounded by the laws of probability or reason, while the legitimately injured side, the wrongly accused, could only allege the undramatic fact of its injury or innocence. The contest, the trial, was, finally, an entertainment, or a trial-by-entertainment, and that he, as the accused, no more enjoyed the presumption of innocence than had any unpopular man at any time.

The trial, in his case, was an inversion of the formula: he was, more than assumed, more than adjudged (denied the possibility of error carried by that form), he was *known* to be guilty. He *was* guilty, and the trial existed to prolong his entertaining punishment, and to ratify that entertainment under another name.

The Puritan Ethic led to the American hypocrisy of disavowing the need of pleasure. So pleasurable acts were called by the name of Service to Some Higher Good, their pleasurable nature denied, and that denial defended to the last—the gauge of a public act's pleasurable component, in fact, could be said to be the extent to which its performance was decried as onerous.

In 1854 a Jewish child in Bologna fell ill. His Catholic nurse, concerned for his immortal soul, secretly baptized him.

The nurse confessed to her priest, and the Catholic hierarchy heard of the baptism. The boy recovered, but the Bishopric of Bologna, enraged that a now Christian child was being raised by Jews, had the boy kidnapped and hidden away.

No pressure from the family, from friends, from the world Jewish community, from foreign heads of state, could cause the Church to produce the boy.

Even to assert the family's "right" was to give credence to an opposing view. But if there were not an opposing view, the kidnapping would have been stripped of its value as entertainment and stood simply as an obscene depredation.

And now he knew the meaning of the curse.

Memory

The whir of the fan when the girl had stood there became confused with other memory.

The Rabbi had said that as one studies the Torah, as one reads the same portions at the same times of the year, year after year, one sees in them a change; but, as they do not change, it must be we who change.

But each time he thought of the Saturday he thought of the girl, and it was always the same—the whir of the fan blowing the dress as she stood there and asked for her money.

It blew the dress and, with it, an odor of uncleanliness.

And was the smell magnified by time?

For, at the time, he'd thought how he'd be hard-pressed to have sex with her, as she smelled unclean. That was the factor, then, perhaps, which buried the memory; for, when they'd come and asked him, "Do you know this girl?" he said that he did not.

And when they said, "She works on the line," he had not.

"There are so many girls here," he said.

"Waal, this one is exceptionally pretty."

"Is she?" he said; and shrugged. Not to say, "I am beyond that," but, he felt at the time, noncommittally; not to say, "You find her so. Perhaps I, being different from you, may not." No.

And not at all servile, no. Not saying, "You know that I cannot notice your young women," but, he thought, as he looked back, measured, correct, circumspect, not unmindful that it was a—as he put it to himself—"difficult subject," but with a certain dignity, he thought—rightly asserting his right not to be interested. He'd shrugged.

"She was quite pretty," the policeman had said—as if to assert, therefore, what, he thought: that any man would rape and kill her?

No. He had shrugged. And he had not remembered her.

Why had he been disgusted at her smell? Why had he, in fact, noticed her? For she was not that pretty.

"Their notions of beauty," he thought, "are cheap. How could they not be? (To forgive them.)"

But they'd seen it, he realized later. They'd seen it, in fact, before he had. In that shrug. He had not consciously remembered her, but they had read intuited processes hidden from his very consciousness. Could that be?

Yes. He'd remembered her. Yes. Later. And he'd told them all. Everything except the smell.

Except her smell. For he knew, that would be to invite them to hang him.

Her dress looked so limp, so greasy, blown by the fan.

The yellow ribbon tied to the fan fluttered. It was cleaner than her lank blue dress; and why the hell was she looking at him? He'd paid her. Why did she hesitate? What was it to him that she did? And was he responsible for every girl in the plant?

They'd said he had a reputation as a lecher. One girl and then another had reported overtures he'd made. Events which never happened in the world. But they were made so real.

"Their stories are so real," he thought. "And they would die the death before they would disclaim them. I know they would. They would go to the rack before they would recant."

"You, you the Flower of Chivalry. You who've come forth Risking All," the prosecutor had said. Frank snorted, shaking his head at the memory.

What was it they'd risked, who had gained sympathy and notoriety by their lies?

"He came up to me one Saady, and we were going out, by the second floor, and he ast me to stay. So my girlfriends went down, and I thought maybe he wannit to tell me he was going to move me up the line, 'cause I been working there the sixteen months, an' they said after *twelve* months there if you was doin' good they'd move you. But nobody come to me. An' I don't know why, 'cause I'm doin' a good job. So I thought he was goin' to say that they were *movin'* me, when he ast me to stay."

And here she'd put her head down.

Then the Judge, with more concern than Frank had ever heard in a man's voice, as if the whole of the unsure advance over savagery were concentrated in those words, said, "Please continue," then he sighed once and, again, said, ". . . please."

She'd raised her head. Brave, quiet, noble—who would not be struck by her courage, he wondered, except the man who was being murdered by her lie.

"Am I going mad?" Frank thought, remembering. "Well, no. Well, no. It's better. I am better. When I *sat* there though . . ." And, at the thought, he was, once again, in that courtroom; as he went back every day. As in a fever dream.

He was once again in that courtroom, and surrounded by his enemies, his mind destroying him as he sat there.

"Not that they're lying," he'd thought, "and not that

I'm going to die, but that no one will ever know. No one will ever know. No one will ever know," he'd thought. As they'd applauded her. As she stepped down, and the judge cried for silence, and the bailiff cried for silence, but the courtroom knew they did not mean it.

"They are linked by the unspoken bond. Even in this," he thought. "Even in this so-small ritual, where each knows that the other knows, and they are delighted by their part in the play. Delighted by that unanimity.

"The poor fucking swine."

He heard the roaring in his ears, in the courtroom. The timbre changed, as the cheering spectators tried to follow the girl, Alice, the factory girl, as she walked out of the court; and then the crowds out in the corridor began to cheer her, then the crowds on the street. And he could picture her face, her mask of controlled emotion, her humility, her performance of unassuming virtue, of simple honor, unworthy of their accolade but accepting it, in understanding that it was awarded her not for herself but as a representative of Southern Womanhood.

"Yes. As *that*," she said, in her step, in her averted gaze, in her demeanor. "As *that, yes,* I will accept it."

And he could not rise from his seat and kill her— that was the injustice—who'd killed *him*. Who'd walked him that much closer to his death through her perjury. He could not burst down the aisle, duck under the arms of the sheriffs, and move through the crowd in the halls.

Perhaps he could, scurrying like a rat, so quick as to escape their notice, down the corridors, down the stairs, on to the street, where he would find the slut surrounded—wait, but wait, then he'd be free: turning the other way, he could run to the wharves, onto a ship, or out into the country. . . .

A runaway slave's life beckoned to him. He'd sleep in the lofts of barns, and eat—whatever was it that he'd eat? Well, he'd discover it, as he lived. As he lived that life he would discover how to live it. He was small and he was quick and light, and now those attributes would work to his advantage.

He didn't need much. He needed so little, really. That was his secret. That was his strength.

Waiting for his attorney

And there, of course, was the fear of what "they" would
say.

"They" being the Jews more than the Christians; for
the Christians would say anything in any case; and, as
much as one might care for their opinion, there was
nothing one could do to influence it.

"They look at us," he thought, "like we think about
the Etruscans: a strange people about whom we know
nothing."

"The brand of religion you practice"—he framed
his pronouncement in his mind—"can only be called
furtive.

"You are backstreet Jews."

He saw, in his mind, their reaction—the reaction of

his fellow Jews, as he preached to them—mild and won-
dering, waiting, as if there were to be a predicate; "you
are backstreet Jews," and as they found there was none,
they looked away, catching one another's eyes to comment, as on an announcement that fire was hot.

"Furtive Jews."

"And in Leviticus it threatens desolation to the land
if the Jews do not follow their commandments. And it
says that in that desolation the land will enjoy those
Sabbaths that the arrogant denied it. Could that not be
applied," he thought, "—as I'm sure it was applied,
and could say if I knew the Talmud, if I knew the Com-
mentators—to the weekly Sabbath? He Who Does Not
Keep the Sabbath being brought low and, so, forced to
rest?"

He hated the set of his face when he had had and was
conscious of having had what he felt was a profound
thought.

For his face relaxed and his eyes looked down and
aside, and when he felt his face so conform, when he was
conscious that he had been taken, for a moment, away
from himself, he was pleased.

He felt his face, in this attitude, betrayed his new approach to wisdom, and he suspected that it made him
handsome. Momentarily handsome, and he hated himself for the suspicion and for his enjoyment of it.

"Who am I to approach wisdom, and how can it be

wisdom if it is, on the instant, perverted into vanity. How weak I am. How sickeningly weak I am.

"Even, as I do, even to feel superior to the . . ." He wagged his head from one side to the other, thinking, "the relatives." ". . . Who am I to feel this superiority?"

"Now: *study*," he thought. "As they say, 'Who rises refreshed from his prayers, his prayers have been answered.' I wished for a Breguet watch. In a gold case. With my initials worked on the case. And I spoke of it. And my wife bought it for me. The happiness of my possession was marred by the thought that I had angled for it. For it was not a surprise, rather an anticipated fulfillment or disappointment, so how could I look to it without feelings of either greed or anger? I contrived it. I suffered for it. Did the watch keep better time than the Illinois? Or than the dollar Ingersoll? Yes. And then so what? For whenever I looked at it, what could I think, save, 'This is the watch I pestered a woman for'?

'Of such, and of such quality,' I would look at it and think, 'that it never can decay. This is the watch I will have till I die. This is, in effect, *my watch*, and I pushed for it and I achieved it and now it is mine.'

"And now it is gone. They might have told me not to wear it to the jail. My wife might have had it. She might have had it now, and enclosed it in a glass bell on a stand. On an easel. Or hanging, yes . . ." He congratulated himself for not shrinking from the thought. "All right, the word is 'gallows,' and a watch, like anything else, can be suspended. And why, in the name of Christ, should I have worn it at the trial? And why have *glanced* at it, those how many times a day? For what?

"And yet. And yet. And, God knows, yet I could not help myself—as if there were going to be an end of it. When there was never an end of it. And yet I wore that watch. As if the chain were armor.

"And I wore it on the Sabbath. And I worked on the Sabbath, and I broke the Sabbath. What does it excuse me that thousands also did, that my relatives did, or that we never kept the Sabbath. Since our family—"

He looked up at the sound of the wooden door down the corridor, the old green door to the guard's station, as it opened.

He nodded. Out there were the stove and the coffeepot and the deal table.

And the room was clean and pleasant.

He wondered if the guards knew how pleasant it was.

There was an odor to it. There was a smell of coffee, and he imagined he could almost smell the leather of the new briefcase—and hear it squeak—as his lawyer came down the corridor.

The prosecutor

The prosecutor rose to his feet. He lowered his head, and his cheeks moved for a moment, as if he were sucking something out of his teeth. He turned to the jury:

"Let us expatiate upon the properties," he said, "of the Black Race. And let us begin with the words of Scripture. For do we not find it written in Leviticus that if thy servant *love* thee, thou shall *put an awl* through his ear, binding him to the door. And bind him, as it were, to your house for life?

"And I ask you: Why would one submit to that?

"And I tell you the answer you know, which is that it is better than the alternative. Which, to the nigro mind, is not to be conceived.

"To the mind of one bred, nay, born to be a slave, the

alternative is not to be conceived. And you know it as well as me.

"... to venture into the world—a foreign world—unequipped, scorned, no, not for what one *is.* but for the actions one has *taken.*

"I say, further, not for the action's *presumption,* but for its inevitable *discohesion:* resulting in misery for black and white alike, but—and as you hear me I know you will nod with me and sorrow with me—infinitely more oppressive to the black.

"To leave his state? To bear the just wrath of a city disordered—through caprice? Why? Who would desire to do that?

"And, again, we know it's said if every man would act in his best interest this would be paradise on earth.

"And we can, yes, envision nigros who would, through folly, through, as I have said, caprice, would 'quit their master's house.'

"We have experienced it. And what is the inevitable ..."

"Why can I not cease worrying about the factory?" Frank thought. "How strange I am. No, I am a vile man. Incapable of concentrating. Mr. Fowler goes on hours at a stretch, and here I am, brooding over the price of cedar blanks. Price of cedar be damned. I will think of something else. I will think of the Brooklyn Zoologic Gardens, and the behavior of the apes. And I will think how no one can say anything novel about them. . . . " His face brightened. "Except *that!*" he thought. "And Morris said no one could say a thing illuminating or novel about the apes, and here I have."

". . . and *look* at him," he heard the prosecutor say, and he turned his head to see the object being indicated, and he saw the whole courtroom staring at him, and he felt the grin on his face, and knew that Fowler's next sentence would be an indictment of that grin.

". . . while we *sit* here, gentlemen . . ." He saw the jurors nodding. ". . . and he . . . this man," the prosecutor said, "who took that girl, a *working* girl, a *Southern* girl, who wanted nothing more nor better than to earn her bread, and serve her family; who took her, and debauched her, and *killed* her, and hid the evidence of the crime; who had the gall . . . to blame a nigro, yes, a nigro, *mark* you, *also* entrusted to his care; who, by his very presence, and I use the word, gentlemen, by his presence as a *guest* in our state, and our region, *might* have, in humility, *might* have deemed himself held to a *higher* . . ."

"No, but he is *good* at it," Frank thought. "Who could deny him that?"

Fowler droned on, and Frank endeavored to compose his face. "To look away is to acknowledge guilt; to look at them would arouse their anger; to stare ahead might seem to acquiesce in the punishment."

". . . Yes, you may *well* be confused," he heard the

prosecutor say. "Indeed you may. In what may be the *first* display of human behavior we have seen from you, since the inception of . . ."

"The apes. The factory, the cedar blanks, Aunt Bess . . ."

The room stank of sweat and tobacco. The air was still as stone. The prosecutor's word fell heavily, one by one. Frank sat like an animal.

"If he were innocent, he would rise up and kill the fellow," one of the reporters thought. "A man would. *I* would."

Jim

And, one step and then the next. Frank had sat in the court, trusting, as all his family trusted, in some plan or expertise, some strategy or talent, which would, at the end, reveal the prosecution for the monstrous savage lie it was.

But day after day, they argued over the moment that he'd left the house, the identity of the Boy on the Bicycle, the time he had seen Mrs. Breen, and what he had said to her about the parade.

And Frank sat there, thinking, "Yes. This is bad. It's pointless. In each moment the central fact of the case is ignored, the jury is left gazing at me as at a monster. But I must sit here and let justice take its course. For there is a progression, a ritual torment, which, for some reason, it has pleased God to spare me until this point. And if it is my lot to endure the trial, I will do so—as others who were unjustly accused have done before me. I am no better than they. And if it is an initiation—if I can think of it as such—to discover my Manhood, then I will endeavor to accept it as such."

Here his thoughts would resolve themselves into the theme of "Americanism." He would seek and find comfort in his community with both the Judge and the accusers, all connected in the name of Americanism. In the unavoidably impure attempt to find the truth through formal means.

"For if I cease to think thus, then I will go mad," he thought.

And he persevered, day after day. Striving, with all his will, not to look at his watch.

While the prosecutor pointed to him, saying, "There he sits, the monster. *Look* at him: impassive. No grief. No feeling. Not a shade of either remorse or shame upon his face. Barely *cognizant* of the tragedy he has wrought."

And Frank would turn to face the jury, and see them nodding, unconsciously, in agreement. Consumed in this "thing," as he phrased it to himself—this fervor of rectitude.

They looked at him—increasingly, as the trial progressed—with revulsion; and, worse, with self-congratulation for their ability to put their revulsion aside.

They were murdering him.

And how they loved Jim and his testimony.

"Nawsuh, I nevah . . ."

"Did you write that note . . . ?"

"Naw *suh*. 'F I could *write*, I wun't be workin' down the fact'ry, you know. *Temporary*, though I'm glad to . . ."

Here he looked and saw, as he knew he would, the jury nodding in support of Jim's portrayal of the Happy Slave; and, at this particular point, in anticipation, then in approbation, of his ritual injection of submission.

". . . so glad to *have* the job . . ."

"Yes, Jim," they thought, "and this is how a society runs. When each is grateful for his place, and acts accordingly. Will the Strong not nurture the Weak? The White not lead the Black . . . ?

Then who was the outsider? The Kike. The "Nigger to the nth degree"—as the paper had called him—who should have *known* better, having been granted the almost-more-than-provisional status of a White Man. But, yes, they could see it now. In his eyes—to which the papers so often referred. His feral eyes, as they said. His blank look. His lack of remorse. What contrast with this specimen of contrition, this, finally, this *man*, this *Jim*, who, though inferior in race, in intellect, in gifts, in status, still was the equal of all in his dedication to *the idea of the whole.*

". . . and when . . ." Jim paused, and Frank saw the lawyers, the Judge, the courtroom, the world, in effect, wait. Patient. Endorsing him: "Yes, Jim, Yes. We know that it is difficult; and we know, even with our *dispensation,* that your natural *courtesy*—not to say your laudable understanding of your place—inhibits the mention of the White Woman. Yes, but we wait."

". . . and when . . ." Here Jim paused again, his face a mask of humility and confusion. "People," it said, "I am overcome.

"And I know you would bid me continue. And I would please you and do my duty. But I am moved by grief. And know how unfitting, how insolent, how near-to-obscene it would be for me to deign to display my grief for a White Woman. I am lost. Help me."

In memory, here, Frank half saw the prosecutor go to Jim and lay his arm around his shoulder.

It had not actually occurred, but the feeling was so strong in the room, Frank was sure he was not the only spectator who had misremembered it. Jim then continued speaking of the girl. Of how he had seen her, in the week previous, "having soft conversation" with Frank, in the narrow corridor outside the shipping area. Of how Frank advanced and how she retreated, shaking her head. Lost, confused.

Was there ever such a man?

The trial progresses

How could they say Jim could not write?

Frank and his attorney had told the prosecution of the existence of a note from Jim asking for reemployment and they had searched the office, the files, but could find no such note.

Even in its absence, how could the prosecution found its case upon a negative proposition: "No one has seen Jim write, so he cannot write"? But Frank had seen him write, as had his assistants in the office. One by one they were deposed; and one by one denied the existence of Jim's application; not "I do not recall ever seeing such a note," but, "No. It never existed."

It never existed? How, then, did Frank communicate

with Jim, when Jim requested reemployment? They'd all testified he had not come into the office. How did they communicate? He wrote and Jim wrote back.

This was the point Frank tried to make in his conference with his attorney. "Ask them *that*," he said, and, always, the man looked down and away, indicating, "Please do not tell me how to run my affairs. I do not wish to embarrass you by pointing out your ignorance of my field."

But the man was a fool.

Frank saw, now, that that which he had taken for courage was foolhardiness. The attorney had no desire to see Frank acquitted. An acquittal would subject him to the rage of the city. No. He wished to be seen to have made a valiant effort. He wished to have upheld, at great personal cost, a principle—the right to a fair trial.

"What a fool. What a fool I was," Frank thought. "Why did I enter into this charade? What could the man have *possibly* gained from my release? "The fees were poor, and had he 'won,' they might have been his last.

"The swine," he thought, "I can see him now, in his clubs, in his haunts.

"Smug. Sure.

"'That was a fine thing you did . . .' And the man deprecating it. With a sad shake of the head, to indicate 'a sad business.'

"A vile business, but for the principle involved. And

the interlocutor reiterating, '*No*. A fine thing you did.'

He could see both men. In some club. On some veranda. Bursting with self-congratulation. Calling the evil
good. How like the Christian. How like the Christian, he
thought.

Testimony

Of course he'd looked at the girl. How could he not? He was a man. But that was what they'd questioned at the medical examination.

Fowler had talked of "rumors of his deformity and his perversion." What were these rumors? They had not existed until Fowler called them into being.

Then the girls had come forth and alleged, "He could not do it like other men could," and they said, ". . . his deformity," two of the three stumbling on the word.

In what was it supposed to consist? This disgusting, undescribed, and indescribable malformation? That, as the others did, he had ungovernable sexual tastes but, unlike them, was incapable of satisfying them? That he, the

Jew, was the same ravening lecher as the black, but his "performance," unlike that of the black in the Southern fiction, was pathetic—that he was, in fact, a eunuch.

Was that why he'd been elected as the killer, in preference to the sweeper, Jim, who, it was clear, had killed the girl?

For Jim came in a dead man already. He was tried and convicted through proximity to the crime, and by the color of his skin—already sentenced absent the evidence, which served not to indict but merely to confirm and to add the verdict of reason to that of race prejudice.

Jim was already dead. He'd raped and killed the girl, and afterwards scrawled, "I rite this while big blk mans has his way wid me."

"Why would a black man," the attorney prosecuting had said, "why would a *black* man," he said, "try to evade suspicion by writing a note *pointing* to himself . . . ?"

"Why would a man want to *kill?*" the defense attorney said. "The note is *false.* . . ."

"Are you suggesting," Fowler said, "that this nigger, the *sweeper,* as in a *chess* game, thinking three moves ahead, that the man little more than an animal resolved, 'I will kill, I will molest and kill . . . '?"

Here the gallery and the jury and the judge inclined their heads somewhat as they always did at this point in the narrative, in respect for the dead, in solidarity with each other and with the generations past who had upheld the code, the amorphous code, the well-nigh or perhaps completely nonexistent code, to which they felt that they subscribed.

"What is this code?" Frank thought, as the prosecution droned on in that cadence, the substance of which never failed to entrance and delight his listeners.

". . . and what is that *right?*" he thought. "What is that sweetness of which there is no surfeit?" Frank thought. "It is rectitude."

". . . to her death—to her *death*, I say—and wrote a *note?* Had the presence of mind, *barring—barring*, mind you—the ludicrous notion that he had the foresight, that he had the presence of mind, to forge a chain of causation whereby we would think, 'It cannot be Jim did the deed. Why? Because a note exists, written by the girl, and *naming* Jim . . .' But, of course, Gentlemen, the note is a *forgery;* and the *defendant* wrote the note. And so . . .'"

Frank's mind drifted. "What folly the law is," he thought. "What might take its place? Perhaps it exists to prepare us for loss. And for sorrow—the clean promise of which becomes almost welcome after the obscene travesty of the law. And if we are to have cruelty, might we not call it by its name?"

And he saw that for which he wished, that for which he wished in the law was not "common sense" but "paradise."

"I understand rage," he thought. "How comfortable

to have it endorsed by one's peers. How lovely. That the state, that the community, that one's home and religion, all say, "Go forth and kill. In the name of God.' What have they done else these two thousand years," he thought, "with their prattle of 'progress,' of 'the future,' of 'change,' of 'America'? What swine, what fiends, what hypocrites—this American Religion."

"... he wanted me to do it with him," the factory girl had said, "and he made me go into the other room with him, and he told me I didn't do it with him, I'd lose my job, but when we got there, he took down his things ... but he ..." And here she paused, and when the court-room was cleared of the women spectators, and when the judge and the jury and the prosecutor all leaned forward, all quite, as solemn as only prurience endorsed can be, all that she would say was, "He was formed different."

He was formed different. She would say no more. And she wept.

Then they would look at him—proud, vehemently proud of their restraint in not falling upon him then and there and having his life.

Formed different, she said. And the subsequently scheduled medical examination had the city rapt, waiting for news.

His wife

It was the grossness of his wife, he knew, which upset them. Her weight. Well, that was one of life's tragedies.

And it was not—for he thought of it at length—that the association with the animal prompted the comparison; no, he corrected himself, it may have, indeed, prompted it, but it was not at the *core*; for *they* looked like pigs, the men with their pink, rusty, milk-colored skins, and their necks growing out over their collars. They looked like pigs, with their short noses and their cheeks puffed out, and they were fat.

They were fat, with their bellies dropping out and down over the belt, and vast legs, and the slow way that they turned their heads; who considered themselves full of self-restraint (you saw it in their eyes), who turned their heads so slowly as he passed, to say, "Yes. I see you. And

I won't show that I judge you—though you are a fiend."

Full of that vaunted Southern self-respect.

And there was that which was attractive in it. There was that in it he could respect, if it were not so false. So vicious.

He saw it was directed at his wife also. That they looked at her as they would at a sow. And, then, what was he?

For they could not see their lack of fastidiousness, and accounted his fastidiousness priggish or inverted— his dress, his figure; not "dapper," as in some favored one of their own; not "trim," not "slight," not, if one of their own group at the Coffee Corner, "bantam," "Banty."

None of it. He was the invert who did what with that gross woman behind him, behind the rail, sitting and crying. Crying at any hour of the day—at this description, that assertion, from the fatigue, God knows what, from the anxiety, from shame.

At any moment. Continually, preternaturally. Weeping. As the crowd laughed at her, as if she were some animal.

How could they laugh at her? Who spoke of Southern Womanhood? *They* were the animals.

And he supposed it was a blessing, that she was not what they, if it went that way, would call attractive, seductive, oriental, voluptuous—for what would they not make of that, who were so interested in sex, in his sex. In his penis, in his habits. As if he were a specimen captured by savages who'd never seen a white man.

Photographs

If it had been the watch, could it not arguably have been the cardinal? And if it had been one or the other, did that not argue a plan; and, if a plan, then a reason for his trial?

Or, if he'd been chosen at random, then, at least, reason behind a plan in which he had been caught by accident?

And if there was that force sufficient to make such a plan—given he'd been ensnared through no fault or through no error of his own—would that not counsel submission to a power of such magnitude?

Submission, possibly, but not acquiescence, he thought, unless one could discern the reason, or the good, in it; and, even if so, why me, he thought, rather than another?

Absent which answer, submission would become courage, not to say faith.

"How much do we unwittingly intuit," he thought, "in extenuation of that which we lack the honesty to call 'random'? So," he thought, "so, we could argue both sides of the proposition.

"And if there were *no* predestination in the walk, or in the cardinal. Or in the watch, or in myself at all, and all my actions, and my very self, then . . ."

"The Greeks wrote," the Rabbi had said, "'Either the Gods exist or they do not. If they do, then, no doubt, things are unfolding under their control; if they do not, why should we mourn to depart a world ruled by chance?'"

"All right. The watch. The cardinal," he thought. "Yes, these, but what portents did I *ignore*—for surely my consciousness, my capabilities, and my predilections prescribe the choice of my impressions. If I had been ill on that day, would I have stopped by the jewelry window at all? Or might I not have walked to the pharmacy? And what would have happened then? Or if I had stopped at Sloan's for a cigar? Or if I had lingered to watch the cardinal . . . ?"

". . . the *pictures*, Mr. Frank . . . ," the doctor said.

Frank came around. He heard the man repeat the phrase, and his eyes focused, slowly, on him. "The pictures, yes," Frank said. They were of girls in various states of undress. Some having or pretending to have sex with other women, some with men, some simply sitting, looking, Frank thought, quite bored. Drugged, perhaps. He heard the doctor drone on. ". . . your *impressions* . . ."

"What?" Frank said, and drifted away.

". . . *force* you to cooperate?" he heard the doctor say. Then he was back again in contemplation of the cardinal.

". . . or come another day. But I must insist on some, some, some *semblance* of cooperation." Frank drew in a long breath.

"Or do you wish me to go and file this report with the Commission?"

Frank looked at the man.

". . . and say that you've been uncooperative?" the man said.

"I've lived my life as a fool," Frank thought. "Every word and every gesture of my life—those I called Good and those I called Bad—has been the act of a fool . . .

"If there is this vicious stupidity in the world, and I have, to this point, escaped it by chance, by merest chance, thirty years, and accounted my astounding fortune as a show of merit." He sighed.

"A man had as well establish a school in How to Avoid the Plague . . ."

". . . all right," the doctor said.

". . . because he'd had the blind fortune to've escaped it himself," he thought, "and so act as those 'authorities' who have escaped knowledge both of their and others' savagery, and set themselves up as philosophers."

The man closed his portfolio and stood and gazed at Frank.

"I'm sorry," Frank said. "What is it you wished to know?"

"It's too late for that," the doctor said.

"Well, then," Frank said, "please excuse me if I've put you out."

He saw the man look to determine if he was being mocked, and he saw that the man felt he most probably was not, but could not completely dismiss the possibility, and he saw the man decide that dignity was best protected by an angry exit, and he left the room accordingly.

"Where was I?" Frank thought. "The bird. Although I wonder what he expected me to find in those photographs. Or who the men were who created a science of looking at them. Wouldn't any two people, of necessity, have different thoughts and feelings, looking at those cards? And the doctor himself," he thought.

"I wonder what *his* feelings were, in showing them to me."

He rubbed his face. "What can they have been?"

The guard opened the door and motioned for Frank to stand, which he did, reluctantly, as he preferred the room to his cell.

He stood. The guard re-manacled his legs and motioned Frank to leave the room.

Frank shuffled down the corridor. The leg chain ran between his ankles. At its center was welded a second chain, the other end of which was a large ring, which the guard held in his hand.

The guard walked behind Frank. The two moved slowly down the corridor, and through a large metal door, and into the cell block.

"What can he have seen in those photographs?" Frank thought.

"And what would induce a man to take a job like that?"

Examination

They claimed, as their racial due, the right to intimidate, and were outraged when that right was not endorsed.

The way of our race, he thought, has been to agree with their position, and to couch all requests as appeals to their supposed merit.

How insulting the phrase "a credit to his race"; and, equally, "their contributions to the country." What country? And, to turn it on its head, those who would patronize the Jews, what contributions had *they* made, past the accident of their ignorant birth?

What Indians had they fought? What British? What vaccines invented, songs composed, what, in short, had they done except rest content on some supposed inherited merit? Those savage dogs on a dungheap, he thought.

"But nothing will be defended as vehemently as a lie, and there's the truth of patriotism.

"'Contributions,' indeed, meaning, 'what have you done for me?'"

"A Christian country," he mused, "built on the lie 'I am saved.'

"Saved from what? From death, which means what? That they have been rendered immortal? By what? By the incantation of a ritual phrase, 'I believe . . .'

"What pagan idolatry," he thought. "It makes the sin of the Golden Calf charming and mild.

"I am saved . . ." To be proved when?

And can they really believe that their life on earth is worthless? Do they not mean it, rather, of the lives of others?

"Savage, psychotic swine . . . ," he thought.

As they prepared for his second examination.

"And what did it mean to her, 'He is not like other men'? She means, it was some misheard understanding of circumcision. Yet she was unsure what it meant."

His lawyer should have said "Disrobe," he thought.

"He should have had me do it in the courtroom, where it could have been *shown*.

"What did it mean? What can the girl have meant?"

He sat in his cell and looked back on the physical examination.

"Yes, I will. No, I will not. Yes. I will," he thought. "No. I will not. No. I will not think of it."

But he could not keep himself from reliving the humiliation, the extremity which was mitigated only by his sense of wonder.

"If only everyone knew," he thought.

The end of the trial

The power of the prosecutor's case—to the extent it rested on fact—the power lay in the adamantine refusal of all to believe in Jim's intelligence. In their ability to ascribe more than an almost preverbal animal responsiveness to him.

"What contempt he must have for whites," Frank thought.

"He says 'nawsuh' and lowers his eyes. And he raped the girl, and killed her, and is killing me, and evades all penalty and all suspicion by saying 'nawsuh.'

"Jim did not write the note, for Jim cannot write. Who, then, was the only person *capable*, placed at the scene? Who . . . ?" the prosecutor had said.

But there were the letters. There was the black girl

who had gone to his lawyer's office and offered to sell the letters Jim had written her.

The handwriting appeared to be the same as in the Mary Phagan note, "man has his way wid me." And Jim had signed them. There it was. There was the man proved a liar.

"Then," Frank thought, "if there were only two who could have written the note, and if the writer was the murderer, and if it were shown that Jim wrote . . ."

But what happened to the letters?

"Love thing, I wants jus to be your man, an . . ."

Day after day, Frank waited. And he waited till the end of the trial. His requests to his lawyer were answered by the same patient nod of the head.

But the letters never appeared, and the trial ended, and he was sentenced to die.

Taken to prison

Whom did one thank when the sun went down?

What could he thank, indeed?

For it was pleasure to occupy his mind with philosophy, or conjugations of a verb, or to make lists. He would list the cities he had visited, the books he had read—the novels of Walter Scott, Charles Dickens, or Anthony Trollope. When he could not sleep he would have the books. And he would hoard them, as he thought of it, the more memorables titles till the end; sometimes, of course, he would forget them—the memorable ones—as he made his list. At two, three, at any hour of the morning, he would be anxious to keep in his mind, in his sleepy mind, the well-known titles, and use them to swell his total.

Saying, yet not saying them, to himself, as he listed the lesser-known works. But the effort preoccupied him. He was anxious lest he lose those bonus titles, as he thought of them, as he made his list. And this anxiety limited his ability to range freely. As a man carrying the armful of kindling cannot bend to pick up the one more stick.

He felt these bonus titles impeded his effort to swell his total.

And, if he were to count them at the end, had he not, efficiently, in "saving" them counted them already?

And, indeed, he felt, each time he employed the device, that it would be better to enroll *at the outset* these better-known books in his list and get on with it.

But he never did. And he felt that it was a stupid exercise, as the effort, designed to distract him—this making-of-a-list—rendered him worried and that much less disposed to sleep.

For there were forty-seven of Trollope's novels in the prison library. And over the months he had read them all, but he never could remember more than thirty, and he strove for these, and, at the end of his memory, berated himself.

The verbs were better. For he told himself there was some purpose in their re-enumeration.

But even with the verbs, he rehearsed them not to impress them on his mind, but to distract himself.

If he did not so muse, evenings, his mind recurred regularly to the moments at the trial when he'd felt most humiliated.

And he could not discharge these memories from, as it were, attendance on him.

Like a scab at which he picked.

He could not help the exercise of his obsessed recitals, nor could he forgive himself for what he felt was his shame in being humiliated.

But work would help, and time would help, and the Rabbi told him the Torah would help.

His other exercise was philosophy.

He wondered, in those nights, if the Torah was given man to serve man or if man was, to the contrary, put upon earth to serve God, and our comfort or even compliance of no account thereto whatever.

And what was strength, finally, but ability formed through repetition—in the fields, with the books, in his memory, in his mind?

He rejoiced when he read: "What is he who conquers a city compared to him who conquers his own nature?"

The despised Jew. The Kike.

The stories that they told about the Jew in prison, on the streets, and in the novels. In each of his books there was the Jew, the moneylender, the Shylock, the figure of fun.

Was it worthwhile to throw the book away at that inevitable gibe, or could one not shrug and say, "For the sake of the ten I will spare the town"? And, so, read on, and obtain the amusement or diversion one contracted for? As in the book before him now "recoiled at the touch of the greasy moneylender's hand, as he counted the bills, one by one, into Phillip's possession—the smile on his face a presumption barely to be borne."

He thought again of the men at the Coffee Corner, in the morning. Eating their roll, their fresh bread roll, and drinking their coffee with chicory.

Thick men, freckled forearms, wide faces, smiling at each other. Smiling. Good, slow smiles, full of that sweetness of the South.

It was not false. It was real.

He'd seen it. Though he'd never felt it directed toward him.

Like circumcision itself, his appearance debarred him from any option of mistake on their part.

He was The Jew, and that was the end of it.

And had he decried it? He had not. At the Coffee Corner, in the court?

At home? At no time.

Then was he so weak as to expect a reward? For the mere performance of his duty, in forbearing? Forbearing what? There was no choice in it.

Well: man was weak. But it was his task, now, to overcome weakness.

No. No. It was not his job to have been born with that capacity.

It was his duty to repeat his efforts in spite of his inabilities. And time would give strength to his operations, but it would not feel like strength. And when he looked back, to compare today with the past, he would feel not pride but sadness. It was this feeling, the Rabbi said, which was called wisdom.

He read the novels, he studied the verbs, he ruminated on philosophy, in prison, where he was awaiting execution for the crime of murder.

The tea

He remembered the tea had tasted like salt.

As he sat at his desk that last Saturday.

The tea had tasted like salt. And he had ruminated
on it.

What could be the cause of that? he had wondered.
Salt in the water, salt in the cup, salt in the tea?

Would they adulterate the tea with salt? Why would
they do that? Perhaps they "cured" it, somehow, he
thought, with that which contained, or would, when put
in contact with some other substance, "create" . . . (Not
"create," he thought, "precipitate." Could one "create"
salt? If the two components were brought into contact
and some agent used to fuse them, had one "created" the
salt? What other word, he wondered, could I use? "Facil-

itate"? Certainly not. Am I not, am I not—yes, he thought, I can reason scientifically. Yes. If others can, then I can. Why not?) Am I not, then (and nothing *but*) a "catalyst"—which is that agent which brings about, *but does not participate in,* combination?

This is what Man is.

The very act of drinking tea.

The very fact of checking ledgers; the fact of ordering raw stock, as ordering the cedar blocks, in which I cause others to perform certain actions, as they, in turn, surely cause *me. . . .*

What a joke. What folly—for now does my tea taste, after all, any the less like salt?

What a shithole.

Oppose me who can, for, in the keep of my mind, he thought, I am, if not free, then . . . then, he thought, less limited than I am outside its confines.

"Miz Scholz," he then called, "could we try once again with this tea? In fact, please, could I have coffee?"

"Well, we must advertise, and that's an end to it," he thought.

To whom could he be thankful? And for what? Who aided us? They persecuted us. We strove and have endured in spite of them. Did they not persecute us?

Does that deserve out thanks?

And if, in an atmosphere of possibility, in a land of plenty, we thrived; if, free of persecution, one has managed, two have managed, and thrived, was this not the principle upon which the country was built? To let the individual thrive, to let him pursue his goals of peace and, should it be, prosperity? Was this not the purpose of the founding of the country? So I say: If you have succeeded, you have done so through efforts of your own. If you were not impeded, those who ignored you did no more than was their duty as men.

If you were aided, why should you not have been? Were you not entitled to it, as were those who aided you?

This country is not God. You need not worship it. It was established to free men from the tyranny of kings, and it is our right here to pursue happiness and live in peace. Our right. Should a child prostrate itself in thanks that its parents have not beaten it?

And was that child an orphan, how much more were they beholden to treat it with care.

Am I in error? Show me where.

The work clothes

One never got wholly free of the stench in the prison clothes. Even when washed—perhaps especially then—they assaulted him with the stink of cheap soap and dirty rinse water, as if the stink was not washed out but fixed by the weekly ablution.

He tried to school himself to identify that new-washed odor as "clean," but he could not do it. The clothes were filthy. The stench was geometrically compounded by the effort to hide rather than remove it.

"I am too sensitive," he thought. "Most live with bad unpleasant odors all their lives. Why should I moan because I, for a time, escaped it?"

Pleased with his philosophic construction, he shook out the ash-blue clothes and laid them on the bed.

They were stiff with the laundry starch. He thought, as he did every week, "If I could only wash the starch out, and hang them to dry in the sun . . ."

His blue clothes . . . "Not blue," he thought, "not blue." *White.* Not grey. Ash white. Ash grey. Blue only by courtesy. Washed-out blue grey. Ash grey. Perhaps the color of stones on some far-off beach. Uninteresting stones—not those the traveler would remark, but those he overlooked.

"People with eyes this color must be killers," he thought. "There is such a thing as 'killers' eyes,' that's true. That's certainly true. We must not credit the things we read in books. They all are advertisements. We must only trust the things which we have learned.

"Does it always come through pain?" he thought. "Well, *those* lessons—there may be others, but *those* lessons are incontrovertibly our education. Those lessons exist beyond the power of anyone to talk us out of them. Like a stumbling against a hot stove.

"Who, however deranged, would do that again willingly? Perhaps nothing less mechanical than this is education.

"But what, now, would I do differently?

"Believe in no one. Trust no one. Do nothing to set myself above the crowd. Confide in no one. Hope for nothing at all; arm myself, kill those who would torture me. Why must I submit to their obscenities in the name of some law? What is the law to me? I thought that it was my shield. When it protected me I 'believed' in it. What can that have meant? That I voted for myself."

He looked at the work clothes laid out on the bunk.

"Not the 'Negro' smell," he thought, "not the fresh washing mixed with sweat. Not the heat of the iron, but clothes as if they'd been boiled in shit." Exactly as if they'd been boiled in shit.

He shook his head.

Nothing, he thought, will be defended as vehemently as a lie.

The food

Someone of his friends had something of a diet in which he refrained from a few foods and lost the weight he'd wanted without effort.

"I simply eliminated alcohol and dairy and sweets and bread," he'd said, "and I shed the weight. Eleven pounds in two months, although during the time, I had been traveling in Europe."

Well, it was an issue, Frank thought. His wife was fat. As was her mother. And his father was fat. And his grandfather.

His uncle, who had told the story, had been traveling in Britain, which, Frank thought, lessened the merit of his fast, as who had ever praised Britain for food?

He thought about his uncle's pride, and wondered

how much of it had to do with action contrary to what, for want of a better word, he thought of as "Jewishness."

And, if the people were gross, if they so thought of themselves, was it not caused, this condition—if the condition was the thought or if obesity—by their displacedness?

Aha, he thought.

Though slim himself, though slender, though disposed to equate it with royalty, and though disposed to feel superior to his relatives, over those he knew, Jew and Gentile alike, who fretted over their weight, he fought the urge to consider himself chosen; and he wondered: might it not be a fear of the outcast? Might it not be the self-loathing, he thought, of the displaced—that their very metabolism would not function to allow them to assimilate food in a foreign land?

"The very foods we eat," he thought.

The jailer scraped his key along the bars as he came down the gallery.

"Yes, All right," Frank thought—and there was something comforting in the sound.

"'Royally slim,'" he thought, "although I know they called me sickly. And turned on me for it. Slim. Slight. Slender. Girlish." He shuddered.

"Or, in Arctic climes," he thought, "*there* it would be a disadvantage definitely. Where the body's urge to put on flesh would serve one. And the opposite not do one well. But in the *South . . .*"

Down the row, there was a quick conversation in undertones. The guard and a prisoner down the row, talking.

The guard responded, not unkindly, from the tone, to the request, whatever it was. Then Frank heard another brief exchange—almost an exchange of pleasantries—between the two, and then the guard moved on, dragging his key on the bars as he moved from cell to cell for the evening lockdown.

"But in the South you would think it was an advantage," Frank thought. "*I* always found it so—not to be disposed, for example, to *sweat.*"

The guard was at his cell, and he heard the key rasping on the bars, and then the quick tack-*thik*, as the key went into the lock. And then he was locked down for the night.

"No. I will not think of fire," he thought. "In fact, its opposite is Cold of the North, and the Eskimos I have just fortuitously touched upon. Though they themselves are slight. But muscled. And disposed, I think, to brawn. To a brawn tempered by cold—so that, perhaps, it's accurate to call them slight.

"I would think they're of a type similar to their dogs, as both have been bred both by the *climate* in which they live and by their exertions *in* that climate."

He tried to think whether any species fell outside of this description, and could only offer himself, transplanted.

———————

They were late with his food.

"All right," he thought. "I have to learn the difference between defending my position and promoting my interests."

"I am entitled to my food, and a case could be made for demanding it on time *this* time, to ensure compliance in the future. And that would be an attempt—for who can say it would succeed?—to defend my position.

"But would it promote my interest?

"First," he thought, "Is it worth fighting for? And, then, is it worth . . . No. No," he thought. "It is all contained in the first question. That is the question: 'Is it worth fighting for?'

"That is the question of the philosopher who is not afraid to seem foolish. Who is not afraid to be thought weak. Who can rest content with his own opinion of himself—for it is *myself* I must conquer, and he who conquers himself is due more praise than he who takes a city. For if I can still my longing to be thought well of, then . . .

"And I am not hungry," he thought. "Finally, I don't want the food now. I do not require it. I *require* to be thought well of.

"Then what kind of beast am I—for they have kidnapped me and will surely kill me, who would strive to defend his—no, I will not say it," he thought—"*manhood* by demanding the food be brought him at the appointed time.

"Are all quests for recognition similarly vain?" he thought; and, as he did, they brought the food.

One man opened the cell, while the other man stood back with the pump shotgun. The man with the tray came in and set it on the bench. As he bent down, he flicked his eyes up to look at the prisoner. Then he backed out, and the cell was locked. Frank heard the two men walk away.

"He smells of cabbage," he thought.

"The cell still smells of cabbage, and it's from that fellow. Looks like a sausage. And where is it written I must love my neighbor?"

He looked at the tray. He picked the small bench up and put it next to his bunk. He sat on the bunk and began to eat.

"No. Where do we find we must love our neighbor? No. We must *treat* them well," he thought, and found that he was pointing, as if in a disputation. And he wondered if it was a "Jewish" gesture, and a "Jewish" trait. And he wondered, "What does that mean?" And he thought, "You know what that means."

He ate his meal, happy to find he was hungry for it.

His books

"And what can it mean that he gave his only begotten son? If he had a son, where was his wife? And is that not idolatry? Where is his wife? No. I'm sorry.

"And the difference is here: *Abraham* did not kill his son. *Their* God did. And the difference is 'God so loved the world,' where *we* are not told 'God loved the world'; we are told to love *God*.

"And we are not told we should love the world. And perhaps it is the love of the world which leads to murder, where the love of *God* . . .

"'Abracadabra,'" he thought. "'I create as I speak.'

"It did not ward the plague off. And in *Les Misérables*, we see it in their chain letter: 'Little White Paternoster, save me from . . .'

"'But if I am to have wisdom I must pass beyond hate,' one voice said. And the next said, 'Why?'

"Is it an advance to be told to 'love our enemies'? Who does so?"

He looked down at his plate.

"And some food goes slowly and some goes fast. But if you leave it on your plate it will rot, and the more complex the organism, the quicker it will rot and the worse it will stink. What does that tell us?" he thought, and, "How many processes were used to stamp this metal tray?" He examined it.

"Only two," he pronounced, and nodded. "And the name of the maker part of the second.

"No. I lie. For the initial stamping makes *one*, to gain the shape, and I would not venture to combine it either with the impression to give the depth nor with turning the rim. So say three, and the stamping of the name part of the second. What is business but fore-thought?"

He mopped up the sauce with his bread. He wiped his hands on a handkerchief taken from the back pocket of his dungarees.

He rose and sighed and moved the small bench back to the wall.

He took the tray and its utensils and placed them on the floor near the bars.

He turned and looked at his books.

There was the Hebrew primer. There was *Les Misérables.*

There was the Torah, in Hebrew and English. There were three novels by Anthony Trollope. There was the notepaper and, there, the several pencils.

Behind him were the bars.

"Abraham refrained," he thought. "I'm sorry, but that's true."

He picked up a piece of notepaper, folded it double, and used the corner to clean a space between two teeth. Then he sat on his bed.

"Oh, Lord, I'm tired," he thought.

The Rabbi

"There seem to be two courses," he said, "though they both may be one. But I do not think they are."

"Go on," the Rabbi said.

"The first is to do these things to better ourselves; or to become . . . I don't know how to say it, but the end, I think, is to become . . . the words I might use are 'fuller,' or 'wiser,' or 'more *happy*'—I think that those are the words—through the things that we do.

"The second, for want of a better word, is 'to serve God.'" He looked at the other man. "What do you think of that?"

"There are many ways to serve God," the Rabbi said.

Frank's face fell.

———

That night he thought about the Rabbi.

"Well, what was he but a man? An overworked man, out of goodness or, perhaps, if he was paid for it, out of necessity—but lump them together under one head and say, 'from a sense of duty'—working as a prison chaplain.

"A tired man, of necessarily stock responses. He was sent not to 'share my enlightenment' but *to enlighten me*—which, in fact, he does. Through his unconcern. It is not to him, but to *me*, to reason," he thought. "Why should he care for me at all?"

"He, I am sure, in fact, has prejudice against a man he cannot but think guilty. Ah." He nodded.

"Guilty and 'Bad for the Jews.' What could be worse for the Jews than I? What could be worse?"

"And perhaps, to suffer in silence is to Sanctify the Name.

"What trash runs thought my head," he thought. "What nonsense.

"What effort there is in weaning oneself from the world. We can succeed for one second, then we are drawn back into it. Briefly, briefly, free of regret. Free of our anger. For a moment. And then drawn back into it. All those beasts . . ."

He thought he saw pictured before him the courtroom, and the faces of the reporters, transfixed in perfect completion. Perfect in their happiness, in their submission in the Tribe—as Levites assisting the sacrifice.

"You swine," he thought. "You Christians."

A skill

The process of learning a foreign language seemed to him the paradigm of human endeavor.

One struggled in the darkness; and mastery came—when it came—in increments so small as to be recognizable only in retrospect.

And accomplishment carried no particular joy, only a feeling of irritability. As, he thought, of *course* the word for "eternally" in Hebrew was *tamid.*

"Further," he thought, "to whom could I boast of my mastery of Hebrew? The Jews would take the ability as a matter of course, and no one else would care."

In learning, one said, "I will know it in the future." But that particular future never arrived, for the term—in its use here—meant "the present."

"Not *a time to come*," he thought, "but a magical, simultaneous present. Like this time in all respects save that in it I will speak the foreign tongue.

"For who would pine for a time to come which was remarkable only for the fact that time had passed, in which passing time one had suffered to master a skill?

"No," he thought, "the future is simply idolatry. And, similarly, 'Change', and 'tomorrow.'

"Equally the past. For that is how they've condemned me—in the search for a magical past, like the present in all respects but with no Jews.

"They long for some magical past when there was no strife; and point and say, 'If he were gone, this past would reappear.'

"So this past is, again, the future—for even if one could return to it, when would one do so but in a subsequent moment? So, it is the Magic Future, free of strife, in which the Goyim will be freed from their historic impediment, and in which, equally, I will have mastered Hebrew, and the seven forms of the Hebrew verb.

"Well, then," he thought, "how can that future exist in which, at once, I have mastered Hebrew and there are no more Jews?

"Clearly no *one* future can exist, for all are, to a certain extent, at least potentially contradictory; or, say, 'mutually excluding'; and so, it is not the future at all which one seeks, but (in a supportive proof) *idolatry*, and, so, it is proved.

"Which does not help me with the following verb: *shin hay mem*, to guard. *Shamoor*, guarded. *Shomer*, guarding. *Nismor*, guarding, or protecting, oneself.

"How peaceful it is here, he thought.

The Hebrew language

The Rabbi took a packet of tobacco from the pocket of his shirt and began rolling a smoke. He offered his hands toward Frank, who nodded, his thoughts far away.

He finished rolling the one and then the second cigarette. He handed both across toward Frank, who took one.

The Rabbi took a kitchen match from the same pocket of his shirt and struck it on the side rail of the iron cot. The smell of sulfur filled the room.

"Why does it make the heat less?" Frank said. He looked at his cigarette.

"Does it? I think it *does. . . .*"

"'F you thought of it . . . ?"

"I *think* . . . ," the Rabbi said, "that it *distracts* us. . . ."

The men sat there smoking for a moment. Then the Rabbi raised his eyebrows to say, "Well? Shall we continue?" Frank nodded, and they bent over the books, spread open on the cot.

"*Zachor*," he said. "To remember. *Lecket*, to glean. *Shamar*, to guard. *Nagah*, to touch."

He continued. The Rabbi leaned back in his chair, to take his body out of the sun. There was some cool in the wall of the cell, and a small triangle of shade between the wall and the bars.

"*Ahav*, to love. *Shatah*, to drink. *Hain*, favor, or grace. *Maskoret*, reward. *Azav*, to leave. *Amrim*, sheaves. *Poal . . .*"

Frank's thought went back to the trial, as always. Not his arrest, or the assault that day on the streets, not his incarceration, but the trial.

"Was I naive?" he thought, as part of his mind thought most of the day, every day; and, "Was ever anyone so naive?" He rebelled at the presence of the other man in his cell, as if, now, as his thoughts recurred to the trial, the other man were witnessing his degradation.

He looked at the shadow on the floor. The window bars, across the joint in the flooring, told an angle of thirty degrees, or two o'clock. In half an hour the Rabbi would leave. But how, he wondered, could he get through the half hour?

"Yes . . . ?" the other man said.

Now the cigarette was hot, burnt to his fingers, and

the smoke was hot in his lungs. He took the coffee can and pushed the butt into the sand in it and held it toward the other man, who shook his head and then inclined it toward the book, to say, "Let us continue."

Frank was overcome, at that moment, by his hatred of the Rabbi—by furious, overwhelming hatred for him and for all that he represented.

"No," he thought. "No. Wait. No. Wait. What am I going to do now? Kill him? What? *Kill?* Measly little Jew. Sour sweat. What is he, *sweating* into his cheap suit?

"Why doesn't he take his *coat* off?"

The Rabbi was speaking.

"*What?*" Frank said. "*What . . . ?*"

"*Moledet,*" the man said.

"*What . . . ?*"

"*Moledet.*"

"*Birth.* Birth." Frank said. "*Birth.* Kindred."

Shalat

There was no talk of a pardon, he was told. It was enough, he was told, that the governor had commuted his sentence to life in prison. That man would never again, he was told, hold elective office in the state; and was, in fact, he was told, in danger. He had received threats. He . . .

Frank dozed somewhat, as his lawyer went on. he heard the references to "years to come" and "eventually"; and he drifted off, and, in his mind, this haze mingled with his sleep in his cell; and the lawyer seemed, in his dream, to be using a Latin term, and that term was "salt."

"Assault?" he wondered. *"Soult?" "Saut?"* The root was familiar, but he could not apply it to the present case of his incarceration.

"And why should he speak in foreign tongues?" he thought. "What is the purpose of it but to obscure?"

But perhaps it was Hebrew, he thought, in his dream. The *Leshon HaKodesh.* The Holy tongue. "Salt." He reduced it to *Shin Lamed Tof.* "What can this root mean?" He dreamed, in his dream, he was in as stone building in some Eastern port city. He was dressed in a toga and carried a roll of papyrus, or what he took papyrus to be, as he walked into the building which he then knew was a library. But there were women there, which struck him as odd, as he knew that women, in the city in which he found himself, in ancient Greece, in Rome, perhaps, would not have been allowed into the building.

"Not *women*," he thought. "*That* was not the operative prohibition. It was *Jews.* Jews would not have been allowed. "*I* would not have been allowed. . . ."

During the day, he thought back on the dream. He progressed. From "What was I seeking?" to "some word," to "some legal term," to "sue"; and, thus, to the memory of his encounter with the lawyer the afternoon before, and, thus, to its reiteration in that evening's dream, and, unbidden, later, to the word "salt."

But was it Hebrew? he thought.

When his work in the dispensary was finished, he returned to his cell for prayers. And, after prayers he took down the lexicon, and a pad and pencil.

"*Shin. Lamed. Tof,*" he wrote out. "Or, *Shin. Lamed. Tet;* or, *Samech Lamed Tet* or *Tof*" he wrote. "Or . . ." Here he looked at the list and perceived these would be enough for his beginning.

Under the first he found nothing. Under the second, "*Shalat. Shin. Lamed. Tof:* to domineer. From the Aramaic: to overcome, to prevail."

Could that be it? But, no—as it solidified, and became not an unexplained experience but a landmark, and that landmark only the one meaning, and that meaning unconnected to his dream, he discarded it. It was devoid of mystery. That mystery was the word "salt," which he had dreamed, and which was being brought back to him to remind him, to admonish him. But of what?

And, suddenly, he was back in his kitchen. On that Saturday morning. Over his breakfast. Sitting alone. Early. Ruthie out shopping, as she did Saturdays, his wife asleep upstairs, and he was in his kitchen, cooking porridge. He was reading the newspaper. His hand went out for the salt, and the glass jar knocked over, the cork fell out, and the salt sprinkled over the counter.

"That," he thought, "was my first premonition. If I had one. As I look back to it: that was it." And then he thought, "There is no augury in Israel, No sorcery in Judah," and, "Thou shalt not suffer a witch to live," and, " . . . no signs or portents."

But surely the Torah contradicted itself on this point, as it did on most every point, giving alternate or conflicting advice or commandment.

Were there not, he thought, Medad and Eldad, whom Moses himself allowed to prophesy? And was there not . . .

"No," he thought. "This is new to me, and I should

not be allowed to confute even *myself* in this ancient argument. . . ."

("Nadah and Abihu," a descant ran in his mind.)

" . . . and *Baalam*," he thought. "Whose prophecies were directed by the Lord. And . . . and the Prophets *themselves*," he thought. "Ezekiel, Elijah *himself*; and, further . . .

"I must ask the Rabbi" and "The man knows nothing" warred in his head. From the short conflict emerged: "What can you expect of a prison system so poor, so savage; and from a man who *himself* . . ." The conflict reemerged with: "No, I will not think ill of the Rabbi, who, whatever his incompetencies, has worked to help me.

"The salt was *spirit*," he thought. The feeling grew as it came back to him. " . . . and I thought, 'scrape it up and throw it over your shoulder.' and then I thought, 'that's superstition, and unfitting to a man who can understand the workings of cause and effect.' And then I thought . . ."

He remembered how he prided himself on his logical process: "I am a careful man, and am I to fly in the face of ancient custom (which would not exist without a reason) without first examining it? For my desire to perform magic with the salt is strong."

And he remembered hearing his wife stirring upstairs, at that early, unaccustomed time, and hoping she would not come down to spoil his cherished Saturday morning privacy.

"Why might it exist?" he thought. "That superstition? And could it, in any way, affect the progress of . . ." Here he remembered the boy riding past on the bicycle, and here, too, that the day was the Confederate Memorial Day; and that he might have difficulty with the crowds on his way home from work.

He had swept the salt with the fat side of his hand, toward the counter edge. It formed small, diagonal ridges in the moist day, adhering to the wood; but he swept it along, over the edge, and into his other palm, as he debated.

He wondered how he would act next—puzzled that he could divide himself in two: the actor and the observer at once; and the actor again into two: he who would throw and he would not throw the offering; and then it came to him, and he raised his left hand, and held it over the porridge pot, and threw the salt into it.

"I have not wasted it," he thought. "It has meaning."

But what was that word?

He glanced down at the pad and saw, written there, *Shalat.* He tried to remember its meaning, and found it was gone.

"No, it must be there," he thought. "For it was there a moment ago. *Shin. Lamed. Tof. Shalat:* to . . ." "Yes?" an opposing voice asked. "Yes," he thought. "To overcome. From the Aramaic."

A different religion

There was something in it. However he tried.

There was something in it . . . just beyond him; he knew what it was when he did not confront it intellectually.

When he looked away, as it were, there it was. It was a warm and correct feeling of belonging. "That is it," he thought. "It feels 'correct.'"

It was a "clean" word, he thought.

But when he confronted it *beyond the issue of faith*, there was little he could see.

When he confronted it, he saw that they did not want him and despised his efforts to belong. He saw that, to them, he would always be a Jew. And that all his ratiocination regarding assimilation was, to them, pathetic. More, that there was but a short step between their sad bemusement at his antics and their rage. But beyond that, he felt, there was something in it that he—not "as a Jew," certainly no, but "as a man"—was entitled to. Something that They had.

That something was his right as an American. That was his right as a citizen of a country which guaranteed religious freedom.

What was that freedom, if not the Freedom to Choose?

Oh, but the smallest movement could have meaning. Not only the larger signs, oh, no, the smaller signs too—and, perhaps, more so.

"There is a different religion," the Rabbi said. "It is no more complex than that.

"Medad and Eldad," said the Rabbi. "Yes. Nadab and Abihu.

"The question of prophecy. Where were we?"

Americus

What was "the Country"? Frank thought. There was no country. There was but a loose association of common interests cloaked, for convenience, in the mantle of a civil religion.

This religion was the highest authority, to transgress against which was death.

That was, he reflected, a democracy. This was democracy: the rule of the Mob. The Mob had elected itself God, and worshiped itself under another name. That name was America. "But," the Rabbi said, "the dove had been dispatched the three times. Once, it had returned. The second time, it returned with the branch in its mouth, and the third time, it had not returned at all.

"Could it not be," Frank reflected, "that the dove had

wanted to remain on the ark? That when Noah expelled it, it returned hurt, hurt and fearful; that when he sent it out again, it returned with this evidence: the land exists, but it is bitter.

"Here, I bring the representative fruit.

"Then, when Noah repulsed it again, it went forth, having been given no choice but to make its way in that bitter world.

"*Marah*," the Rabbi said, "is 'bitter.' It survived in Latin and the Romance tongues as *amer*, which we see further elaborated but essentially unchanged in the map-maker's name Americus and in the land America."

"Vast ships upon the sea," Frank thought, "brought starved men, clothed in armor, to the wonder of the brown-skinned natives.

"And the well of Miriam," the Rabbi said, "followed the Israelites throughout the decades in the desert. 'Miriam' is also from *marah*. And also the well is *meribah*."

"The ark," Frank thought, "thus becoming also the Garden of Eden. From which they did not wish to be expelled."

". . . and in the modern 'Mary,'" the Rabbi said.

"For the land," Frank thought, "the land is bitter."

Visiting day

He turned the ring on his finger as he waited for his wife.

"Yes," he thought, "I know I am doing it."

He remarked the prison smells, and tried to sense them as she might: repugnant, fetid, revolting, the sewage smell—that nameless poverty and despair and sewerage and sweat which was in the wood, which so revolted him at first.

"That was the worst trial," he thought. The clothes imperfectly cleaned and, then, ironed, the stink burned into them.

That smell. The stench of shit on everything.

"Is it an actionable luxury to be clean," he thought, "and should the clean atone for their mindless enjoyment of magnificence? What must she think, to come here smelling of soap, her very dress clean?

"In the desert, the air was dry. Smells did not carry. Everyone was washed in sweat. Everyone's diet and life was the same, so odors, when they came, went unremarked; or, if remarked, were not improbably recognized as the smell of home.

"Not unlike the furniture polish on the hall hatrack; for a nomadic people have only each other. That is their home."

She came forward, the lawyer at her side. He watched them.

He noticed he had stopped twisting the wedding band.

He stood and caught the eye of a guard, who nodded to him.

He walked the three paces forward to the wire mesh, and waited for his wife. His finger held the place in the grammar book.

Songs

He walks with me, and he talks with me
He tells me that I am his own.
And the joy we share, as we tarry there,
None other has ever known.

The words came to him on the breeze from down the prison yard, and they seemed sweet, like the breeze. The words seemed natural, as the discovery of some previously unsuspected force, some force which underlay the conscious world, and moved it.

Like the force of love, as it's discovered to an adolescent.

Or the force of fatherhood, where one says, "Now. Ah. Now I understand"—Where so much unclear becomes clear, and we see understanding is not a reordering of opposites in the mind but the clarification of apparent contradiction into simplicity.

"Yes," he thought. "Clean as the breeze and fecund like the breeze. Like the spring field: the notion one is saved—that one has but to embrace salvation and one is saved.

But the fallacy—the Rabbi had said—lay in this: One cannot award oneself salvation. The joy one feels in doing so comes from usurpation of the power of God.

In linking salvation—whatever that might be—to faith, one sets oneself the simplest of tasks and, upon its completion, awards oneself Godhood. Of course that feels good. "How could that feel otherwise than good?" the Rabbi said. To have illicit sex, or rape, or murder, sanctioned by Authority, that felt good too. "Any idolatry," the Rabbi said, "that is the force which sent you here.

These saved folk have been convened these two thousand years to kill and hate and call it good.

Of course they're wedded to it. What savage ever denominated his barbarity other than Reason?

"Of course it feels good," the Rabbi said.

"And tell the drunkard his vileness is a religion, and the dope fiend his lack of control is blessed. . . ." He paused.

"We do not know what is right." the Rabbi said. "We are incompetent to distinguish it. Our eyes lead us astray.

Our heart leads us astray. That is why we are bonded to follow the *mitzvot:* what else do we have? The delusion of comprehension, which leads us to proclaim we are God.

"We understand *nothing.*"

"Of course you're drawn to their songs," Frank thought. "You fool."

"And so drawn to the singers of the songs, and their supposed 'community.'

"And do you think they would have you if you embraced them? You are an object of scorn. Why? Why? It is not for you to say. Do you hear? It is not for you to say.

"Stand guiltless before God—to the extent you can—and let the Christians behave as they will. You cannot stop them.

"You cannot join them. Why would you want to?

"Study, live, and die."

But the song came through the window: "I walk in the Garden alone . . ."

"To be a man," the Rabbi said, was to behave as a man in that situation where there were neither the trappings nor the rewards of manhood: scorned, reviled, abandoned, humiliated, powerless, terrified, mocked.

"*Now* be a man . . ." the Rabbi said.

The song came through the window. and as he denominated it strength to resist it, to that extent he felt strong.

The dot

Who would know that the dot had not been placed on the i at the time the word was written?

What process, he wondered, what forensic magic, would reveal it?

For he had no doubt that such methods existed; or, if they did not, that they would come into being at some future date.

For it was on that most powerful entity he pinned his hopes—upon that benevolent God he knew: when he referred to it by name, it bore a name too simple and mundane to compass its clear awesome power. Its quotidian name, the Future.

In the Future, methods would exist, he knew, to reveal all that had been hidden.

Methods would exist—for, no, we could not feel that they existed now. (Would not their current being detract from any potential redemptive aspect of their discovery? Yes, he thought, it would.)

Such methods would—though the groundwork might be allowed to have been laid (for what can build on nothing?)—have to come to light in years to come, brought into being for some other task; not, he knew, certainly, for the purpose of examination of his life, or of this letter; nor, perhaps, for the analysis of ink at all, but for some unconnected application. Then, he thought, at some point it would be discovered, as a matter of course, that such methods had a wider use, had many uses, one of which was the dating of ink.

Then, when the arcane became the open; then, at that golden time, the time of the Future, of Progress, of Change, of Heaven, in fact; in that time, then, when the processes existed, when the black ignorance of the present had been cleansed through a simple perseverance . . . then, yes, the technology would—he could not doubt it—exist to date the ink.

Then they would know that his confession bore a secret, different and, perhaps, in a way, more mysterious and deeper than the Simple Secret of his Soul—whatever that might be.

He'd fought with it.

Though driven by the urge to purify himself, though driven in each sentence, at each word, to speak the truth, he knew he lied. Every word, he thought, colored by the wish to defend, to extenuate, to distract. ("To distract whom?" he thought, but continued.)

In any case, to attempt both to cleanse and to defend himself, he wrote of his pride, and of his arrogance, and of his dishonesty in social dealings. He wrote of his off-hand treatment of his wife, and wrote and wrote. At all times thinking, "I could continue transcribing these 'sins of character' interminably. For I know them to be true as they are endless. My sins are endless. But I am not cruel."

And as he thought it, he wrote it:

". . . mistreatment of those around me. And sloth." But I am not cruel.

His written confession continued.

As he wrote, he was troubled by the reference to sloth.

For he knew himself to be hardworking. Not, certainly, like the factory hands, no. But hardworking. Dedicated, in fact. In the area, the administrative area, of his operations.

And not cruel.

Here, again, he was troubled, in a way different from that occasioned by his assertion of industry. For he knew he'd written the denial of cruelty for the eyes of some person or power in the future, which would have interest in him solely—he would have to admit it—as he was convicted of killing that girl.

And they might interpret this, his freewill confession, as a sign of his guilt.

They might—might they not?—magnify what he thought of and was ashamed to realize he thought of as his "flaws."

No, no, his disingenuousness, his candor in the frank confession of his sins, was, and he knew it was, an arrogance.

And he might, he knew, in fact *be* guilty of those very sins the confession of which induced him to think he was pure of.

But not of cruelty. No.

And as he wrote it, he felt that he had transgressed. "I am not cruel," he wrote, and felt that, here, the mechanism was inverted.

For he felt, in the heart of himself, that he *was*, in fact, not cruel. He had known cruelty, and had seen it, and could not recognize it in himself. But as he wrote in his confession "I am not cruel," he felt the mechanism thus: Yes, but I have transgressed in the transcription, and my assertion must mask a cruelty of which I am unconscious.

He looked back up the page.

He saw that the *i* of "insight" sloped into the *n*, and that he had not dotted the *i*.

Though he knew that the word was clear enough from context, and was, in fact, most legible as it stood, he took the pen and put a dot over the *i*, which, through the delicacy of his touch, achieved the character of a minute flowery rhombus.

"Who would know," he thought, "the dot was not placed on as I wrote the word?"

As he raised the pen, he admired the apparent unity of the dot and the letter.

He could not, "even in possession of 'the facts,'" as he thought, see any inconsistency of color or form in the two.

"Someday, however," he thought, "the science will exist," and sighed. "But what would induce one to apply it in this case?"

He thought, "And what would it accomplish?"

He sat up, his feet on the floor, sitting up straight on the bunk. His confession on a writing board on his knees.

"Why would they ever be moved to examine it?" he thought; and, "The secret will die with me."

Punishment

"It says throughout," the Rabbi said, "that they are blessed who bless us, and cursed who curse us. I believe our history has shown this is true."

If there were a God, Frank thought, then that which has befallen me could not be random. If it were ordered, then, surely, I could determine a cause-and-effect relationship between my actions and my trouble.

But here, he thought, he committed the error of an egocentric theology. For could not and *must* not God's objectives be different from his own? "*Must* they not differ?" he thought; and, again, "If I assign a reason to my trials, such reason beyond my comprehension, do I not, *again*, suggest myself, in my very punishment, important to God?

"But then, perhaps, I *am* important to God, but my happiness is not. Or, perhaps, my happiness is not, but my welfare *is;* and He, whatever power He is, construes the second more important than the first. Like a good father—or, for all that, like a bad father also.

"A man," the Rabbi had said, "a poor man, found a fine horse upon the road. 'How fortunate you are,' his friends said. 'Well,' the man said, 'well, you never know.' His son took the horse out to ride, and was thrown, and was maimed. 'How misfortunate you are,' the friend said, and the man said 'Well, you never know.' But the next day the recruiting officers came round, to press the Jewish boys. Where they would go to the Czar's army to serve twenty-five years. But the man's son was maimed, and so he was spared. 'How fortunate you are," his friend said, and the man . . ."

"Yes," Frank thought. "In *fact,* that is true."

Gematria

The Hebrew dictionary was his passport to another land.

"If I had a photographic memory," he thought, "I'd have but to glance at it—but where would be the merit in that?"

And he felt a kind of self-indulgence, a sumptuousness, in fact, reading through the words, knowing he could not retain them, that they were his for the moment only.

"There is that of cultism, of the Mandarin, in the perusal of the ancient, accidental text," he thought. "For though it has come down to us in this form, the form was, we would have to say, arbitrarily fixed, and errors in the typography have been canonized and studied.

"On the one hand, could we not extrapolate truth

from an error? Gregor Mendel did. And, on the other hand, might we not be as likely to arrive at nonsense, and, aha, are these two cases not in fact equally likely outcomes of the study of Scripture?

"Having arrived at that, how have I spent my morning?

"Might we not study *any* text? And where would that lead us?"

He signed. He swung his legs down to the floor and looked at the floor, and then up at the bars. Cast into the bars was the manufacturer's mark: "Ginnett and Hubbard. Penal Engineering. Booth, Ohio."

"Let us, then," he thought, "lay this out upon a grid."

He counted the letters and found forty-two.

"If we add in the punctuation marks, we arrive at fifty, which is five by ten, and may be arrayed thus:

```
G I N E T        N A L X E
T X A N D        N G I N E
H U B B A        E R S B O
R D X P E        O T H X X
                 O H I O X
```

The word NALXE presented itself to him. Turning the first block through ninety degrees, he saw the word AGROO in the second square, and his mind caught upon the phrase "The letters of the First Square suggest themselves to me as more probably containing reason than those of the Second Square. But perhaps this is a trick played on me by the inevitable connotation of hierarchy in the terms 'first' and 'second' square." He studied the squares, and rotated them to form diamonds, yielding:

```
        G
       T I
      H X N
     R U A E
     D B N T
      X B D
       P E
        A
```

and:

```
        N
       N A
      E G L
     R R I X
    X A S N E
    O N X L E
     X A D
        O
```

And he realized he had come to suppose and expect that the squares would resolve themselves, and that even this consciousness would not dispel a conviction that they would do so.

```
        G
    T X X N I
    R U A E
    D B N T
    X B D
    P E
    E
```

He began to translate.

"God, the (thy?)—xnn, ruae—Dobent? Dabent? . . ."

It would require work and, obviously, dedication, but given both, meaning would, he was sure, be found.

"But why," said the voice of reason, or, as he thought of it, "a detractor," "would a message be impressed into the bars of a cell?"

"There are two reasons," he thought.

"One: It seems that any science is the attempt to wrest meaning from the superficially random. All great advances in the fields of . . . ," he thought, "medicine, chemistry, and . . ." He was reluctant to include physics, as he was unsure of precisely in what it consisted. "Surely, physics, though, whatever it contains, must advance through the connection of previously unconnected facts, else what is the good of an equation?

"Most of human thought, in fact," he thought, "is the attempt to find a hidden meaning. My second assertion is this: If the meaning does not exist, then there is meaning in our attempts to create it."

"This assertion on my part is either very wise or foolish," he thought. "What of a grain of sand? And what fool would be fool enough to study it? And yet. And yet . . . And yet there exists such things as *crystals*, and many have learned from them.

"Now: four men went into the garden, we are told— Azai, Ben Zoma, Aher, and Rabbi Akiba. One became mad, one took his own life, one became a heretic, and one, Akiba, went on to glory as a Teacher of the Soul. Now: Could that very garden be contained in these squares? Why not?

"Or else, in what did it consist, save in the arbitrary arrangement of matter which they believed would hold a secret.

"Will I say that these men, Hubbard and Ginnett, were put on the earth to place their names upon that bar to instruct me? No. I will not. Will I say *I* was not put upon the earth to find a meaning in their names? I cannot discount it. For is that not the enterprise in which I find myself? And, if it's ludicrous, how much more so is my incarceration for a crime simple right reason knows me innocent of having done? And if I may assume that it is not ridiculous to state that there *may* be reason in the words on the bars, then may I not extrapolate that it is not beyond the realm of reason to assume that those men had been put upon earth *in part* to furnish the material of my investigations?

"Now, I know that to be false, for I cannot fix myself

as the center of a universe which, aeons ago, gave rise not only to the alphabet but to my disposition to reorder it in equilateral components. There is nothing in *that*—I cannot go *that* far.

"But now I am lost, and to what must I cling in order to both navigate through and gain instruction in the Garden?

"What if I were to look once again at the names in the bars, and to discover that I had misread them?

"What if it pleased God to keep me in this cell for sixty years, and I employed the time to create a cosmology based on the meaning in those words, and *after that time* I looked once again and found I had mistranscribed them, and all of my elaborations were based upon error—would not that error have meaning? And if so, meaning sufficient to justify my—we must say—misguided efforts?

"And if the error were *not* misguided, of what use the original words upon the bars? And if they have no worth, why do I find myself studying them?

"Is it, then, the exercise of my capacity that pleases me, and the notion that it has significance merely the goad to that pleasure?

"Perhaps it is our gift to reason merely to the extent which would outwit the beasts of the field, and any further or greater employ or elaboration of that gift must lead to evil.

"And then, perhaps, it is the purpose of what we have

come to call 'pursuit of knowledge' to countervail the exercise of that evil propensity. Could that be the case? And then, perhaps, it is the meaning of 'knowledge,' 'to do no evil,' and that is why it pleases.

"For how can we posit an ultimate Good, or own an Improvement, as we know we are both bound to die and likely to inflict misery during our life?

"But surely there are medical advances which have lessened pain and lengthened our lives.

"But again, perhaps, if we would follow out thoughts to the end, it is a greater good to pass quickly and be done with it. Can we say that without demeaning that force which gave us our life?

"Would it be better if those two deluded men, Ginnett and Hubbard, who divert themselves in what they choose to style 'Penal Engineering'—would it be better if they had not lived? If they had not lived, I would not be drawn to this line of reasoning. Has this reasoning made me better, or worse?

"Better or worse for what?

"To what end?

"*Beth-Lechem*," he said. "House of bread. The breadhouse. Certainly the home of a baker. *Elizabeth*, God-is-my-pact. *Daniel*, God-is-my-judge. *Bethel*, the house of God. *Salem*, Peace. He looked at the Hebrew primer in his hand.

"'Who rises refreshed from his prayers, his prayers have been answered.'"

Palestine

Palestine, then, was a dream.

Not peopled by Turks—who- and whatever they might be—but as in the days of the Bible, when tribes of white people, just like oneself—Westerners, in fact, he thought—roamed through a desert which might seem to us inhospitable, but which they found a comfortable home. The desert was home to them. Hot, but dry, during the day, cold at night, granted, but was not the one a welcome respite from the other? And could one, *did* one, not experience it as a comfort, wrapped in the rugs and hides, so warm, so light for transport, which made it home?

What did one need, finally, but the few things one could carry?

"I am of a wandering race," he said. "The world is my home."

Had not the Rabbi taught him, "*Arami Avodi Avi . . .*"? "My Father," as the creed had it, "was a wandering Aramaean, who went down, with just a few, to Egypt, and, there, became a Nation."

Each time Frank thought of this passage, he felt conflict.

He loved what was the first instance of his ability to appreciate Hebrew poetry, in the alliteration of the first three words, but he felt shame, as the word "Aramaean" conjured to him the image of a blond, a non-"Jewish," finally, a *Christian* man—as if it were the purpose of the creed to claim, as he thought, more distinguished, or, more to the point, less "maculate" heritage.

"No. They'd have to be dark," he thought, "for the sun was hot. To be light would be to be maladapted. What could *that* avail? Nothing," he thought. "And my brief notion of life lived in the open must confirm the simple truth that it is better to be correctly adapted than to be in fashion. Whom would see you there? And what is it but idolatry to crave fashionable appearance in the wilds; where not only is there no *mirror* but, yes," he thought, "in the desert, and distinguished from 'the woods,' there is not even that stream or that accidental pond which would allow one to gauge one's reflection."

At this, he became frightened.

"Would that be, then," he thought, "as if one did not exist?

"And what might that mean?"

He pictured an unhappy, discorporeal existence, which, in his mind, meant nothing but anomie, an existence consisting in nothing but panic, with no external manifestation of what might, for want of a better word, be called the world; and, at once, the complementary 'happy' component of 'not to exist,' which was a free-flowing animal consciousness of joy in oneself and one's surroundings.

So he mused, picturing the desert. In his dream, it was a happy woods, on a low and rolling ground—much like the grounds at the Grand Hotel in North Carolina, where he and his wife's family stayed summers.

"That was the desert to him—a state of perfect balance, where he was neither hot nor cold, hungry nor full.

"But not a state of peace," he thought. "One of 'equilibrium.'

"But the sun would start to go down, then where would I be? I would gravitate to my camp—to my Desert Camp—where there would be a tent in the woods. This tent would be laid inside with fine Turkey carpets. There would be a fire. Within, a small ring of rocks, and a brass tripod over it, and a young girl cooking for me and the smell of coffee.

"She would look up to me as I entered, her eyes soft

with submission, her eyes grave with love. 'A woman of my tribe.' Yes," he thought. "Yes, I can allow myself to revel in that phrase. Who is to stop me? 'A woman of my tribe.' But," he thought, "she would not have a hooked nose."

———————

The lights went out. He was alone in the dark, with the smell of sweat and filthy men's bodies. At intervals, the wind would shift for a moment, and bring him a breath of the fields.

"I suppose that this filth is just another form of fecundity," he thought, "but I can't think so.

"Soon I'll be asleep. Perhaps the Christians are right, and we should take all we have and give it to the poor. If they would, I would."

His vision

"The question," the Rabbi observed, "may be asked in a different way."

Looking back, one could always devise or imagine warnings or signs; but, as they had been unheeded (if, in fact, they ever occurred), of what good had they been? What could they do save comfort one after the fact with assurances of omnipotence?

"That is it," he said. "We can both suffer and mourn, 'How was I to know?' and, at once, celebrate our omniscience: 'I had a sign. Which I did not heed.'

"The argument is, of course, useless. For if there were a sign, why did you not heed—and, if you did not heed, was it a sign?

"What can we not find in our memory to serve our

vision of ourselves? But we can use this instance to confront idolatry."

The Rabbi bobbed his head, and he moved closer to the table, and he frowned across the table at Frank and continued.

"The *essence*, you see," he said, "is a belief in our own power. For if we believe in it *at all*—in our power to overcome what we might call 'chance'—if we are unable to understand our powerlessness, our mortality, then we denominate ourselves God.

"If we are God, what can we not do? We are permitted all.

"Our difficulty lies in accommodating our *weakness*, eh?, into the theory. Our *weakness*, which we see each day and in each aspect of our day—our difficulty lies in *accommodating* this knowledge with the belief that we are, in effect, God.

"And, so we say, 'I *knew* that it was going to rain today. I should have taken my umbrella!'

"Well, then, finally, why *didn't* you?

"Why didn't the man, who proclaims not only that he had the choice but that the choice was superfluous, as he possessed—*beyond* the power to choose—possessed Perfect Knowledge?

"Why *didn't* you take the umbrella? He did not, do you see, as he did not know that it would rain.

" 'Ah', but you say, 'an observant man, eh? Perhaps a

farmer, a man who understood . . .'" The Rabbi shrugged. "Uh . . . 'The *sky*, the *weather* . . . surely he may have known it would rain.'

"Then why didn't he take his umbrella?"

He looked at Frank, as to say, "I am a man without guile, without defenses. And at the moment I stand before you unarmed. Resting solely on the proposition: Do with me as you will."

"Do you see? Which is true? 'Ah,' but you say, 'perhaps there were countervailing motives.' Yes. When are there not?

"The man looked at the sky. He *perceived* it might rain. He chose not to *encumber* himself.

"Or, who can say, the umbrella had been put away. And he was rushed. And unsure of its location. Or perhaps he felt it *shabby*, and his duties of the day . . . You see my point?" The Rabbi said, "Or, or, perhaps, it was too fine, of too fine . . ." He searched for the word. ". . . a *manufacture*. And, similarly, that it would be inappropriate to carry it among the people he would see that day.

"Perhaps he wanted to *wrong* himself."

He cast his arms up, to say, "Are we not mature men, and should we shrink at these things?"

"Perhaps he'd had a fight; and, thinking it would rain, looked forward to the very utterance 'I have seen the better path, but I take the worse,' and wished to inflict pain through the . . . the *objectification* of his self-hatred.

"And perhaps none of these is true, and he'd only wished, truly, to've had power over forces powerful over him.

"Who is to say?

"It remains: If he had had the choice, why did he not exercise it?

"If he'd not had the choice, why did he make the assertion?

"The human mind is fashioned to *compare*." He paused.

He sighed, and took a package of cigarettes from the lapel pocket of his coat. he offered one to Frank, who nodded and took it.

The Rabbi took one, and drew a kitchen match out of his pocket. He put his hands on the table, the match sticking up between the fingers of his right hand. He looked down at the crumpled pack of cigarettes lying between Frank and himself.

Frank glanced at him. "How can those," he thought, "who are not Jews understand Jews?"

The prison library smelled of old paper. The scent of hot pine came in the window, as if a sheet, drying in the wind, had billowed, and let the air pass. The Rabbi let the match fall onto the table. He took it and scratched it underneath the table's lip, and he lit both their cigarettes.

"You say that you had a 'vision' on that day. A 'vision' that you should not have gone to the office.

"Well, then, *perhaps*," he said, "you should not have gone."

He shrugged.

" 'What is a dream? What is a vision? What is real?' These are, perhaps, questions for the secular mind. Do you see? For when you come to know all that is real, what then?

"First, whom would you tell? And, then, would you be happier? And, finally, is such knowledge necessary to serve God?

"Torture yourself if you will. The fact is, you *did* go into the office. The question may be asked, not, 'Was it my imagination,' but, 'Of what is my imagination a product?' "

The library

But perhaps there was such a thing as the goddess Nemesis.

And could it be that one was punished not for having more, but for an awareness of it?

Was he meant to act, then, like a Christian disciple, and give all he had to the poor?

The Christians themselves didn't act that way, and they were enjoined to. How much less appropriate, then, for a Jew? And, as he had not been so directed, why was he being punished?

For the voice said, "You have too much."

And were there not many, many more prominent than he, richer than he? More rich? "Hell," he thought, "more rich. I was not rich at all. Am I to be persecuted because I am not *starving?* I didn't set the wages, nor the hours, and there are places within ten blocks of the factory where the girls are treated far, *far* worse. . . ."

"No, the day did not drag," he wrote to his wife, and, "Yes, there is a satisfaction in the order of the day. I am sure that the Appeal will prevail, and I do not write that merely out of form, nor from false hope, nor out of belief in some eventual triumph of goodness or reason, or of balance in Human Affairs—though such might exist, in fact, and I don't discount that possibility, neither embracing it, as I say, naively.

"No. I believe the Appeal will prevail, as I hold that there is a rhythm, if you will, in human intercourse, which one can see in politics, in business, or in any interaction. I see that one violent moment gives rise to its opposite, as a wave dashing on a rock, or as a sudden surge, out of all reason, in the price of a stock; or in the adoption of a style in dress.

"Violence must engender its opposite. And the rush to conclusion, absent any fact (in our case), must, given time, cause, if not an equal, a substantial outpouring of—I may say—equally unthought-out sympathy (of course I will be happy to enjoy it).

"I feel it as one feels a change in the barometer; absent all other signs. We sense the shift in human affairs with an animal sense; and I know it will be so here.

"Already I see it in the attitude of my jailers, and, more significantly, in that of my fellow inmates, who, little by little, but perceptibly, cease to look on me with that unconquerable loathing of prejudice, and commence to see me as a man.

"Perhaps I imagine it; but, no, I do not. Just yesterday a fellow told a joke, and, as I meant to move away—not to seem to wish, uninvited, to presume to be part of the group to which he intended speaking—he gestured (in the minutest way, but there was that communication nonetheless) that I was to stay.

"Which I did. Gratefully. For these are not small acts. They are, to the contrary, that by which our history is woven.

"Which brings me back to the issue of Jim; and an incident which transpired a year ago. Perhaps more. Say, a year ago, when he was leaving work, and I joked . . . (It was a Saturday: Is that ironic? No? Is it significant? No. Probably not, but how could I, at that point, fail to remark it? I could not, I don't think.)

"I joked that he seemed in quite a hurry to be gone—as I would have joked with any employee, I think. For who would not be glad to be off? Anyone on Saturday. I accept it and avow their right. For why should they stay one moment longer than those for which they had contracted? And I have . . . I will not say 'searched my soul,' but 'considered' it, and do not feel at all that I implied anything in the least recriminatory, although it may have been the very license of financial authority which made my joking onerous.

"In any case, I joked that he must have had a full

night planned; and I saw his eyes narrow, and perceived that he thought I had intended it in a suggestive way, which, before God, I did not, and I saw that he resented it 'full sore'; as if my position permitted me pleasantry which, had *he* employed it, might result in penalty—perhaps in a severe penalty—to him. And I allow that, and would not, for the world, have offended him—but I saw that he was angered and that he'd remember it.

"A man wrote that we should be slow to hire and quick to fire—that if we saw an employee would be trouble at some point, we'd better discharge them then and there, paying whatever was necessary to the end of whatever contracted term, but get them removed from the premises before their attitude . . . (And, of course, our attitude toward them—for who could function with suspicion? Suspicion is the heaviest weight—that cumbersome anxiety, '*Will* they be obstreperous?' and so on) . . . that we should remove them immediately, as the cheapest course. For if we see or suspect that they *might* cause trouble, that suspicion constitutes trouble in itself, which cannot be borne in a well-regulated business.

"When I saw his eyes, I felt, frankly, I had wronged him. Though *I did not intend to;* and although I regretted it. But one of us—well, no, I will not be facetious, I will not say, 'One of us would have to leave.'

"*He* should have gone. I should have dismissed him. And I think, perhaps that I kept him on out of a feeling of *obligation,* as I had subjected him, as I saw that he felt, to ridicule.

"The Rabbi reminds me that we do not believe in false gods, nor in prophecy. And this comforts me, for I am disposed to wonder at the power of the 'goddess Nemesis.'

"As I said. But sober reflection, in light of the Rabbi's words, reminds me that she is nothing but an elaboration of my human feeling that if I had acted differently, all would be well.

"And I know that nothing I have done has brought on this occurrence—that I am not sufficiently powerful, nor is my happiness or lack of it of sufficient moment to the world, to engender this chain of events. To think so is to aggrandize my importance. I see that it is Idolatry.

"My disposition, in spite of that knowledge, to the idea of Nemesis is not magical; nor is it indication that she does, in fact, exist. It is, I know, a simple human urge to accept the attractive lie and call the power of its attraction Truth."

He nodded to a Trusty shelving books on the far wall.

He laid the pen down on the wooden writing board. The board was scoured by years of use. "So smooth," he thought. "And how could it become smooth other than through use? It could not."

As he mused, the man to whom he'd nodded left the shelves and walked behind him, drew a knife from his shirt, grabbed Frank's chin from behind, and cut his throat.

The hospital

Beyond the window there was fairyland. He tried, but he could not dispel the illusion. It brought him back to his youth; beyond youth, to an infancy. He looked and thought, "This will pass quickly, and I will be touched at the quaintness of my thoughts," but it did not pass.

He stood looking and thought, "And I cannot even call myself 'fixed,' or 'mesmerized,' but I do not want to move."

The light was blue grey, and the moonlight shadows were grey brown.

"It is so bright," he thought, "that, as they say, I could read a newspaper by it." He tried to think of a print so small as to thwart the moonlight, but he found the thought too mechanical to grace the scene, and left it unfinished in respect.

The view was soft. The shapes were soft.

"There is nothing in the world," he thought, "equal to this."

He tried to imagine animals as shapes moving in the blue light, but he could not. "It is empty," he thought, "of everything but spirit."

Now, in his cell, he recurred to that night by the lake.

"How perfect it was," he thought, and, "What were my worries? What sick folly would have caused me a moment's unrest then? Could I but recapture that time . . ."

And yet he told himself that could he return, he would, in days, in months, certainly, resume his previous ways—return as he put it, "to myself."

There was the ripped pain in his throat. He could still feel the knife where the man had cut him. He remembered, with a strange shame, thinking, "Why, it isn't even sharp."

He felt the itching which meant that the wound was healing. He remembered the sick, rank sweat in the man's coveralls when the man straddled him and grabbed his hair back to expose the neck and cut his throat, and the look in his eyes of calm happiness as he cut his throat.

"What is more lovely than belonging?" he thought. *Nothing.*"

"Once a month the moon is full and stays full for how many days, and then ebbs to nothing. And at every stage it can be beautiful or stark, or it can fill us with dread—there is no saying what concatenation of circumstances might produce what effect. The man who tried to kill me looked as if he could have been participating at his daughter's wedding, or at the confirmation of a child. Or the receipt of some reward.

"Does perfect innocence exist? What good is it if these crimes are committed in striving to return to it? Should we not simply repudiate it?

Should we not simply avow we cannot return?

"For if we are lured to return to innocence through sin, should we not say, 'I am incapable of distinguishing it, so I will renounce it'?

"Or he could have been a child going to sleep; or on the edge of a perception, when he raised the knife. He held it with the blade extending back, out of the little-finger side of the hand, and back almost parallel to the forearm.

"Who would *know* to hold a knife like that when you did a murder? Where would one *learn* that? Who would *teach* that?"

He smelled the carbolic, and the iodine, soaking the bandages on his neck. He turned his head to the side and saw the white-painted metal of the hospital bed, and, below the paint, the iron.

"White-into-black, and black-to-grey," he thought.

"The paint, and the chipped margin, are not various. But the iron is. That is because it is not man-made; for, try as we might . . ."

The moonlight made its usual flat and long shadows

on the infirmary wall. "As they are moved to the right, it is turned morning," he thought. "And today will be hot. All of these people have been told by their God that it is a praiseworthy act to want me dead. Am I in a dream?"

The panic rose in him. It was checked by the thought: "It was the stock quotation—that was the print so small it would have been difficult to read by moonlight," and then he surrendered into madness for a while.

The scar

His throat healed with a speed which surprised him.

Under any circumstance, he thought, I would have been pleased with my resiliency, but coming as it did, however, in the midst . . . Well, he thought, I was meant to live, in this instance, and that is the truth of it. Had I been meant to die I would have died. And spring, no doubt, and summer have much to do with the process, for is it not true that the sap, that the emotive instinct, that the urge to mate, that everything, in short, is quickened in the spring; and why should we think ourselves exempt?

His scar itched with a force he'd described to himself as intolerable until he reflected he could tolerate it, and that it signaled his life—that he still lived, and that he was healing.

We wish for philosophy, he thought. It will not come, and when it comes, no doubt, we reflect it cost us too dear.

Or I could be miserable, he thought, and lie here reflecting on my misery—which is an equally supportable position.

As an exercise, he began to enumerate and to attempt to embrace his troubles.

By which it will be seen, he thought, if my content (he would not dare to think of it as happiness) is the accident of a momentary amnesia of my plight, or . . .

He listed his troubles to himself, feeling foolish, both for squandering a moment's peace and as their bulk was, to him, almost comic.

For who could credit it, he thought, a man who lately fretted over . . . ? He searched for a triviality from his late life with which to taunt himself.

And I know, he thought, that that mechanism to dispel my rage is close at hand, and it is this:

Perhaps I *was* the murderer.

With this thought, his play was ended, and he fell from philosophy to depression so swiftly as to erase the memory of his investigation.

Nothing remained but rage and fury.

Perhaps I killed her. What was to have stopped me? Nothing at all. Who was to know? I could have killed her, and no one the wiser. And I had the opportunity, and the motive, as they say, if I am that beast, if I am that invert, and would I not be, if I had killed her?

Then the one event, if I had misremembered it, could make it right. If I had killed her, if I could avow the fact, then it would all come right. I would be saved. And that is what the Rabbi meant when he talked of the Christian Outlook.

Then I would be saved.

How would that be? How would that alter one, if I walked down the street a member of that Community? If I confessed?

. . . but, again, how could that be, if I had killed the girl, he wondered, how could it be that a man would merit his neighbor's love more as a murderer than as a Jew?

In the transition to sleep, he balanced the two opposites.

Is there a rendition of events in which I am not a murderer? Is there a version in which I am not a Jew? And how can it be that I do not seem able to shed that identity?

Perhaps they're right, and it is a "blood guilt"— whatever that may be. And they claim they can make atonement for *their* sin by some "confession of faith"; but I cannot; for if I embraced them, they would not embrace me, however far I would go. *Though* their savior was a Jew . . . and if I were to see before me . . . He pictured himself in robe and sandals, in a desert scene, on a hill, preaching.

. . . to see before me those who were *troubled,* those who were *confused,* those who . . . those who were . . .

The breeze smelled to him of dates, of "sand," of the East.

He closed his eyes and saw a deep burnt orange—the color, he thought, of peace.

Each breath was a joy. He could feel it descend to his belly. It thrilled him. In his nostrils, in his throat.

He woke coughing blood, and rolled on his side, groaning.

The blood trickled from his mouth onto the sheet and pooled on the sheet.

He nodded, slowly, in a colloquy with himself, as if to say, "Yes. That's true; yes, I know that's true."

The ride

They took him by force from the prison hospital. Twelve men in three cars. They made him lie on the floor of the first sedan, a bag over his head, and drove through this town and that for the better part of the night.

They talked curtly, and in abbreviated phrases, of their object and their destination, and then the time would pass, and they would lapse, forgetful, into a normal speech, and revert to their everyday subjects—the crops, or town life, or such—until one or the other would remind the group of their errand.

Well past dawn, they stopped and took him from the car.

They took the bag from his head and showed him the tree, and he nodded at the sizable crowd which had gathered, and which answered his question as to whether the drive was a planned or an improvised event.

They moved to re-cover his head, and he asked them to stop, and removed his wedding ring. He asked that it be returned to his wife.

One of the men stretched out his hand in a noncommittal way, and Frank gave him the ring.

They covered his head, and they ripped his pants off and castrated him and hung him from the tree.

A photographer took a picture showing the mob, one boy grinning at the camera, the body hanging, the legs covered by a blanket tied around the waist.

The photo, reproduced as a postcard, was sold for many years in stores throughout the South.

ACKNOWLEDGMENTS

The Jew Accused

by Albert S. Lindemann

The Leo Frank Case

by Leonard Dinnerstein

A Little Girl Is Dead

by Harry Golden

With thanks for

the kind assistance

and encouragement

of Anita Landa